William Shakespeare's 2 Henry VI, aka Henry VI, Part 2: A Retelling in Prose

David Bruce

Published by David Bruce, 2022.

WILLIAM SHAKESPEARE'S 2 HENRY VI, AKA HENRY VI, PART 2: A RETELLING IN PROSE

First edition. July 26, 2022.

Copyright © 2022 David Bruce.

ISBN: 979-8201126995

Written by David Bruce.

Table of Contents

Dedication

Dedicated to My Sister Brenda

Brenda wrote, "During COVID and when visitors were restricted from visiting their loved one in the assisted-living facility I worked at, a patient mentioned to me how much she liked spaghetti during a late-night conversation we had. She was a night owl like me. Her name was Dee. I called her "Gerdy." Then she would say, "Dirty Gerdy," and we'd laugh. Anyway, on my way to work I bought two spaghetti meals from Olive Garden. I left for work early that night. I went to work, set up outlet dinners in the dining room, went to her room and wheeled her down to the dining room where we had dinner together. At that time, the residents weren't leaving their room and had their meals alone in their room. It was nighttime and everyone was already in bed, so I didn't see a problem. She was so grateful and had enough food for three more meals. It was such a simple gesture, but during that time it meant so much to her and for me."

Brenda once bought a newspaper at a gas station on Thanksgiving and tipped the female employee $5, and the employee cried.

Brenda wrote, "I do remember that. I also remember when George tipped a TeeJays waitress $100, and she cried. Our family does a lot of good deeds all the time: I unload people's grocery carts when the people are in those electric scooters. If they are alone with a few groceries, I'll leave cash for the cashier to pay for the groceries. I've had a lot of good deeds done to me when I didn't have a lot of money. It feels good to pay it forward."

She added, "I just have one more thing to add and then I'm done. I've had a lot of people in my life do good deeds for me when I was at a low point on my life. I was at a low point for a very long time. David, you know what you've done for me, and I can never thank you enough. Martha paid for antibiotics for me when I had strep throat and didn't have money. Rosa bought me groceries. Carla has done so much, and she had us over for Easter just after Chad died. When I say US, I mean all of my kids. She was so sick and ended up at the Emergency Room that same night. Frank gave me a car. And George buys my gas for me whenever he's in Florida. And Mom and Dad were good people. I had a lot of good influences in my life that made me be a good person. At least I hope I'm a good person. I try to be someone Mom and Dad would be proud of."

***

The doing of good deeds is important. As a free person, you can choose to live your life as a good person or as a bad person. To be a good person, do good deeds. To be a bad person, do bad deeds. If you do good deeds, you will become good. If you do bad deeds, you will become bad. To become the person you want to be, act as if you already are that kind of person. Each of us chooses what kind of person we will become. To become a good person, do the things a good person does. To become a bad person, do the things a bad person does. The opportunity to take action to become the kind of person you want to be is yours.

Educate Yourself
Read Like A Wolf Eats
Be Excellent to Each Other
Books Then, Books Now, Books Forever

***

In this retelling, as in all my retellings, I have tried to make the work of literature accessible to modern readers who may lack the knowledge about mythology, religion, and history that the literary work's contemporary audience had.

Do you know a language other than English? If you do, I give you permission to translate this book, copyright your translation, publish or self-publish it, and keep all the royalties for yourself. (Do give me credit, of course, for the original retelling.)

I would like to see my retellings of classic literature used in schools, so I give permission to the country of Finland (and all other countries) to give copies of this book to all students forever. I also give permission to the state of Texas (and all other states) to give copies of this book to all students forever. I also give permission to all teachers to give copies of this book to all students forever.

Teachers need not actually teach my retellings. Teachers are welcome to give students copies of my eBooks as background material. For example, if they are teaching Homer's *Iliad* and *Odyssey*, teachers are welcome to give students copies of my *Virgil's* Aeneid: *A Retelling in Prose* and tell students, "Here's another ancient epic you may want to read in your spare time."

CAST OF CHARACTERS

Male Characters

King Henry VI.

Humphrey, Duke of Gloucester, uncle to King Henry VI.

Cardinal Beaufort, Bishop of Winchester, great-uncle to King Henry VI.

Richard Plantagenet, Duke of York.

Edward and Richard, his sons. In the future, they will be King Edward IV and King Richard III.

Duke of Somerset.

Marquess of Suffolk, later Duke of Suffolk. His given name and surname are William de la Pole.

Duke of Buckingham.

Lord Clifford.

Young Clifford, his son.

Earl of Salisbury.

Earl of Warwick. He is the Earl of Salisbury's son. The family name of the Earl of Salisbury and the Earl of Warwick is Neville.

Lord Scales.

Lord Say.

Sir Humphrey Stafford, and William Stafford, his brother.

Sir John Stanley.

Vaux.

Matthew Goffe.

A Sea Captain, Master, and Master's-Mate, and Walter Whitmore.

Two Gentlemen, prisoners with Suffolk.

John Hume and John Southwell, priests.

Roger Bolingbroke, a conjurer.

Thomas Horner, an armorer.

Peter, his apprentice.

Clerk of Chatham.

Mayor of St. Albans.

Simpcox, an imposter.

Alexander Iden, a Kentish gentleman.

Jack Cade, a rebel leader.

George Bevis, John Holland, Dick the Butcher, Smith the Weaver, Michael, and other followers of Jack Cade.

Two Murderers.

Female Characters

Margaret, Queen to King Henry VI. Before marrying King Henry VI, she was known as Margaret of Anjou.

Eleanor, Duchess to Gloucester.

Margery Jourdain, a witch.

Wife to Simpcox.

Minor Characters

Lords, Ladies, Attendants, Petitioners, Aldermen, a Herald, a Beadle, Sheriff, and Officers, Citizens, Apprentices, Falconers, Guards, Soldiers, Messengers, etc.

A Spirit.

Scene

England.

Nota Bene

Cardinal Beaufort

In *1 Henry VI*, he was known mostly as the Bishop of Winchester.

Strong Supporters of King Henry VI

Lord Clifford.

Young Clifford, Lord Clifford's Son.

Strong Supporters of the Duke of York

Earl of Salisbury.

Earl of Warwick.

King Henry V was born on 9 August 1386 and died on 31 August 1422.

King Henry VI (born 6 December 1421; died 21 May 1471) began his reign in 1422, but he was deposed on 1461; he briefly returned to the throne in 1470-1471.

The Hundred Years War, which lasted from 1337-1453 (116 years), was not fought continuously. The Edwardian War took place in 1337-1360; the Caroline War took place in 1369-1389; the Lancastrian War took place in 1415-1453.

After the Hundred Years War, the Wars of the Roses took place from 1455-1487. In those wars, the Yorkists and the Lancastrians fought for power in England. The emblem of the York family was a white rose, and the emblem of the Lancaster family was a red rose.

We read Shakespeare for drama, not history. He invents scenes and changes the ages of historical personages in his plays. He also changes the order in which historical events occur.

CHAPTER 1

— 1.1 —

At the palace in London, several people were assembled. On one side were King Henry VI, the Duke of Gloucester, the Earl of Salisbury, the Earl of Warwick, and Cardinal Beaufort. On the other side were Queen Margaret, the Marquess of Suffolk, the Duke of York, the Duke of Somerset, and the Duke of Buckingham.

The Marquess of Suffolk had gone to France to arrange a marriage between Margaret and King Henry VI. Now he had returned to England, bringing Margaret with him.

The Marquess of Suffolk said, "Your high imperial majesty gave me the command at my departure for France, as proxy to your excellence, to marry Princess Margaret for your grace. Therefore, in the famous ancient city of Tours, in the presence of the Kings of France and Sicily; the Dukes of Orleans, Calaber, Bretagne, and Alençon; seven Earls, twelve Barons, and twenty reverend Bishops, I have performed my task and as your proxy I married her."

He knelt and said, "And now humbly upon my bended knee, in sight of England and her lordly nobles, I deliver up my title in the Queen to your most gracious hands that are the substance of that great shadow I was as your representative; this is the happiest gift that ever Marquess gave, the fairest Queen that ever King received."

The Marquess of Suffolk had married Margaret only as a proxy. Her marriage was actually to King Henry VI, who said, "Marquis of Suffolk, arise."

King Henry VI then said, "Welcome, Queen Margaret. I can express no kinder, more natural sign of love than this kind, affectionate kiss. Oh, Lord, Who lends me life, lend me a heart replete with thankfulness! You have given me in this beauteous face a world of Earthly blessings to my soul, if harmony of love unites our thoughts."

Queen Margaret said, "Great King of England and my gracious lord, the intimate conversation that my mind has had, by day, by night, waking and in my dreams, in courtly company or while saying prayers and using my prayer beads, with you, my very dearest sovereign, makes me the bolder to greet my King with less polished words and terms, such as my intelligence affords and excess of joy of heart imparts."

"The sight of Margaret entranced me," King Henry VI said, "but her grace in speech, her words clothed with wisdom's majesty, makes me go from mere admiration to joys that cause me to weep. Such is the fullness of my heart's content.

"Lords, with one cheerful voice welcome my love."

The lords knelt and said, "Long live Queen Margaret, England's happiness!"

Using the royal plural, Queen Margaret replied, "We thank you all."

The lords stood up.

The Marquess of Suffolk said to the Duke of Gloucester, "My Lord Protector, if it pleases your grace, here are the articles of contracted peace between our sovereign and the French King Charles VII. This peace treaty for the next eighteen months has been agreed to by both parties: the French and the English."

The Duke of Gloucester was the late King Henry V's only surviving brother. When King Henry VI had been a minor, the Duke of Gloucester had been made Lord Protector so he could rule England until Henry VI came of age. King Henry VI was now old enough to make at least some decisions.

The peace treaty was written in formal language. "Imprimis" means "in the first place." It is used to introduce a list. The word "item" is used to introduce each article in that list.

The Duke of Gloucester began to read the peace treaty out loud:

"*Imprimis, it is agreed between the French King Charles VII and William de la Pole, the Marquess of Suffolk and ambassador for Henry VI, King of England, that the said Henry shall marry the Lady Margaret, daughter of Reignier, King of Naples, Sicilia, and Jerusalem, and crown her Queen of England before the next thirtieth of May. Item, that the Duchies of Anjou and Maine shall be released and delivered over to the King her fa —*"

Shocked at reading this condition of the peace treaty, the Duke of Gloucester dropped it.

"Uncle, what is the matter?" King Henry VI asked.

"Pardon me, gracious lord," the Duke of Gloucester said, "Some sudden illness has struck me at the heart and dimmed my eyes, and so I can read no further."

"Great-uncle Beaufort of Winchester, please read on," King Henry VI said.

Cardinal Beaufort read out loud:

"*Item: It is further agreed between them, that the Duchies of Anjou and Maine shall be released and delivered over to the King her father, and she sent over to England at the King of England's own personal cost and expenses, without any dowry.*"

Usually, the woman the King of England married would bring with her a large dowry. The King of England would be enriched through marrying her. In this case, however, King Henry VI would receive no dowry. Instead, he would hand over to Margaret's father two very valuable regions of land in France. He would also pay for all of Margaret's expenses as she moved from France to England.

Using the royal plural, King Henry VI said, "The conditions of the peace treaty and marriage contract please us well. Lord Marquess of Suffolk, kneel down."

He knelt, and King Henry VI said, "We here create you the first Duke of Suffolk, and gird you with the sword."

The newly created Duke of Suffolk rose.

King Henry VI said, "Duke of York, my kinsman, we here discharge your grace from being Regent in the parts of France under the control of England until the period of eighteen months is fully expired.

"Thanks, great-uncle Cardinal Beaufort, Gloucester, York, Buckingham, Somerset, Salisbury, and Warwick. We thank you all for the great favor done in the favorable reception of my Princely Queen.

"Come, let us go in, and with all speed see that her coronation is performed. She must be officially crowned Queen of England."

King Henry VI, Queen Margaret, and the Duke of Suffolk exited, but the lords stayed behind. They wanted to discuss the peace treaty and the marriage contract.

The Duke of Gloucester said, "Brave peers of England, pillars of the state, to you I, Duke Humphrey of Gloucester, must unload his grief, your grief, the common grief of all the land.

"Did my brother King Henry V expend his youth, his valor, his money, and his people in the wars? Did he so often lodge in open fields, in winter's cold and summer's parching heat, to conquer France, his true inheritance?"

King Henry V believed that his ancestry had made him the hereditary King of France and so he fought a war against the French. After winning the war, he married Catherine of Valois, a daughter of the French King Charles VI, with the understanding that he would become King of France after King Charles VI died. Unfortunately, Henry V died young, before King Charles VI died.

The Duke of Gloucester continued, "And did my brother the Duke of Bedford exhaust his wits, to keep by statesmanship what Henry V had gotten? Have you yourselves, Somerset, Buckingham, brave York, Salisbury, and victorious Warwick, received deep scars in France and Normandy? Or have my uncle Beaufort and myself, with all the learned Privy Council of the realm, deliberated so long, sat in the Council House early and late, debating to and fro how France and Frenchmen might be kept in awe, and had his highness Henry VI in his infancy crowned in Paris in contemptuous defiance of his foes?

"And shall these labors and these honors die? Shall Henry V's conquest, Bedford's vigilance, your deeds of war, and all our counsel die?

"Oh, peers of England, this agreement is shameful! This marriage is fatal, cancelling your fame, blotting your names from books of history, erasing the written records of your renown, defacing monuments — written documents and memorial structures — of conquered France, undoing all, as if all had never been!"

Cardinal Beaufort said, "Nephew, what is the meaning of this impassioned discourse, this rhetorical speech with such detail? As for France, it is ours, and we will still keep it."

"Yes, uncle, we will keep it — if we can. But now it is impossible we should keep it. Suffolk, the newly made Duke who rules the roost, has given the Duchies of Anjou and Maine to Margaret's father, poor King Reignier, whose fancy formal titles do not match the leanness of his purse. He has many high titles, but little money."

The Earl of Salisbury said, "Now, by the death of Him Who died for all, these counties were the keys of Normandy.

"But why does my valiant son, the Earl of Warwick, weep?"

"I weep out of grief because the Duchies of Anjou and Maine are past recovery," the Earl of Warwick replied. "If hope existed that we could conquer them again, my sword would shed hot blood, and my eyes would shed no tears.

"Anjou and Maine! I myself won them both. Those provinces these arms of mine did conquer. And are the cities, which I conquered with my wounds, delivered to the French again with peaceful words? *Mort Dieu*! God's death!"

The Duke of York said, "As for Suffolk's Duke, may he be suffocated, he who dims the honor of this warlike isle! France should have torn and rent my very heart before I would have consented to this peace treaty.

"I have always read that England's Kings have received large sums of gold and large dowries with their wives, but our King Henry VI gives away his own property in order to marry a woman who brings with her no profit."

The Duke of Gloucester said, "It is a 'proper' jest, and never heard before, that Suffolk should demand a tax levy taking a whole fifteenth from the people for the costs and charges of transporting Margaret from France to England! She should have stayed in France and starved in France before —"

In *1 Henry VI*, King Henry VI had authorized a tax of ten percent.

Cardinal Beaufort said, "My Lord of Gloucester, now you grow too hot-tempered. It was the pleasure of my lord the King Henry VI to do that which you criticize."

"My Lord of Winchester — Cardinal Beaufort — I know your mind," the Duke of Gloucester said. "I know what you are thinking. It is not my speeches that you dislike; it is my presence that troubles you. Rancor will reveal itself. Proud prelate, in your face I see your fury. If I stay here any longer, we shall begin our longtime bickerings and quarreling again.

"My lords, farewell; and say when I am gone that I prophesied France will be lost before long."

He exited.

Cardinal Beaufort said, "So, there goes our Lord Protector in a rage. It is known to all of you that he is my enemy. Nay, more, he is an enemy to all of you, and he is no great friend, I fear, to the King.

"Consider, lords, that he is the next of blood and heir apparent to the English crown. If Henry VI dies without having children first, the Duke of Gloucester will become King of England.

"Even if Henry VI had gotten an empire by his marriage, and all the wealthy kingdoms of the west, there's reason the Duke of Gloucester should be displeased at his marriage. A marriage that results in children will keep the Duke of Gloucester from the throne.

"Look to it, lords! Be careful! Let not his smoothing, ingratiating words bewitch your hearts; be wise and circumspect.

"What though the common people favor him, calling him 'Humphrey, the good Duke of Gloucester,' clapping their hands, and crying with a loud voice, 'May Jesus maintain your royal excellence!' and 'May God preserve the good Duke Humphrey!'

"I am afraid, lords, that despite all this flattering, glossy, deceptive appearance, he will be found to be a dangerous Lord Protector."

The Duke of Buckingham said, "Why should Gloucester, then, protect our sovereign, since Henry VI is old enough to govern himself? Duke of Somerset, if you join with me, all together, along with the Duke of Suffolk, we'll quickly hoist and remove by force Duke Humphrey of Gloucester from his seat."

Cardinal Beaufort said, "This weighty business will not allow delay. I'll go to the Duke of Suffolk immediately."

Cardinal Beaufort exited.

The Duke of Somerset said, "Duke of Buckingham, although Duke Humphrey of Gloucester's pride and the greatness of his position is a torment to us, yet let us watch the haughty Cardinal Beaufort. His insolence is more intolerable than all the Princes in the land beside. If the Duke of Gloucester is removed as Lord Protector, Cardinal Beaufort will become Lord Protector."

The Duke of Buckingham said, "Either you or I, Somerset, will be Lord Protector, despite Duke Humphrey of Gloucester or Cardinal Beaufort."

The Duke of Buckingham and the Duke of Somerset exited.

The Earl of Salisbury said, "Pride went before, ambition follows him. Cardinal Beaufort exited first, and then the Duke of Buckingham and the Duke of Somerset followed.

"While these labor for their own advancement, it is best for us to labor for the good of the realm.

"I never saw Duke Humphrey of Gloucester bear himself like anything other than a noble gentleman.

"Often I have seen the haughty Cardinal Beaufort, more like a soldier than a man of the church, as arrogant and proud as if he were lord of all, swear like a ruffian and conduct himself unlike the ruler of a commonwealth.

"Warwick, my son, the comfort of my age, your deeds, your honesty, and your hospitality have won the greatest favor of the common people, with the exception of no one but good Duke Humphrey of Gloucester.

"And, brother-in-law York, you who married Cecily Neville, my sister, your deeds in Ireland, in bringing the rebels back to civil discipline, and your recent military exploits done in the heart of France, when you were Regent for our sovereign, have made you feared and honored by the people.

"Let us join together for the public good and do what we can to bridle and suppress the pride of the Duke of Suffolk and Cardinal Beaufort, as well as the ambition of the Duke of Somerset and the Duke of Buckingham. And, as much as we can, let us support Duke Humphrey of Gloucester's deeds while they promote the profit of the land of England."

His son, the Earl of Warwick, said, "May God help Warwick, as long as he loves the land and the profit and general good of his country!"

The Duke of York said, "And so says York —"

He added in his thoughts, — *for he has the greatest cause.*

Already, the Duke of York was thinking of seizing the crown of the King of England.

The Earl of Salisbury said, "Then let's hasten away, and look to the main chance. Let's keep our eyes on the prize."

"To the main!" the Earl of Warwick said. "Oh, father, Maine is lost, that Maine which by main — sheer — force I, Warwick, won, and would have kept as long as my breath did last! The main chance, father, you meant; but I meant Maine, which I will win from France, or else be slain."

The Earl of Salisbury and the Earl of Warwick, his son, exited.

Alone, the Duke of York said to himself, "Anjou and Maine have been given to the French. Paris has been lost; the state of Normandy stands on a precarious point now that Anjou and Maine are gone. Suffolk arranged the articles of the peace treaty and marriage contract, the peers agreed, and Henry VI was well pleased to exchange two dukedoms for the beautiful daughter of Reignier, Duke of Anjou.

"I cannot blame them at all. What is it to them? What they are giving away belongs to me, the rightful King of England; this land in France is not their own.

"Pirates may make cheap pennyworths of their pillage by selling valuables for pennies, and they may purchase friends and give gifts to courtesans, continually reveling like lords until all they have stolen is gone. Meanwhile the silly real owner of the goods they have stolen weeps over the stolen goods and wrings his hapless hands and shakes his head and trembling stands aloof, while all is shared and all is borne away, ready to starve and daring not to touch what is his own property.

"Just like that silly real owner, I, the Duke of York, must sit and fret and bite my tongue, while my own lands are bargained for and sold.

"I think the realms of England, France, and Ireland bear that connection to my flesh and blood as did the fatal firebrand Althaea burned did to the heart of the Prince of Calydon."

When Meleager, Prince of Calydon, was born, the Fates prophesied that he would live only as long as a firebrand — a piece of burning firewood — that was lying in the fireplace would not be consumed by fire. His mother, Althaea, took the burning piece of wood out of the fire, put the piece of wood out, and kept it safe until much later, when Meleager killed her two brothers. Then she threw the piece of wood back into the fire, and Meleager died as the wood burned.

The Duke of York continued, "Anjou and Maine have both been given to the French! This is cold news for me, for I had hope of ruling France, even as I have hope of ruling England's fertile soil.

"A day will come when the Duke of York shall claim his own, and therefore I will get the Nevilles — the Earl of Salisbury and the Earl of Warwick — on my side and make a show of friendship to proud Duke Humphrey of Gloucester, and, when I spy an advantage, I will claim the crown, for that's the golden mark — target — I seek to hit.

"Nor shall proud Lancaster — King Henry VI, who is also the Duke of Lancaster — usurp my right to the crown and throne, nor hold the scepter in his childish fist, nor wear the diadem upon his head, whose church-like, devout disposition makes him not fit to wear a crown.

"So then, Duke of York, be still awhile, until the right time comes. Watch and be awake while others are asleep, in order to pry into the secrets of the state.

Wait until Henry VI, overindulging in the joys of love with his new bride and England's expensively bought Queen, and Duke Humphrey of Gloucester both fall into quarrels with the peers.

"Then I will raise aloft the milk-white rose, the symbol of the House of York, with whose sweet smell the air shall be perfumed, and in my battle flag I will bear the coat of arms of York to grapple with the House of Lancaster, whose symbol is the red rose.

"And, force perforce, with violent compulsion I'll make Henry VI yield the crown — Henry VI whose bookish rule has pulled fair England down."

The Duke and the Duchess of Gloucester talked together in their house. In this culture, wives called their husbands "lord." The Duchess' name was Eleanor, but the Duke sometimes called her Nell.

The Duchess of Gloucester asked, "Why does my lord droop his head, like over-ripened wheat, hanging the head at Ceres, goddess of grain's plenteous load? Why does the great Duke Humphrey of Gloucester knit his eyebrows as if he were frowning at the favors of the world? Why are your eyes fixed on the sullen earth, gazing on that which seems to dim your sight? What do you see there? King Henry VI's diadem, adorned with all the honors of the world?

"If that is so, gaze on, and grovel on your face, until your head is encircled with the same. You should wear the diadem. Put forth your hand and reach at the glorious gold."

Groveling while lying face down was a part of supplicating infernal supernatural spirits for help.

She continued, "Is your arm too short? I'll lengthen it with mine. And, having both together heaved the diadem up, we'll both together lift our heads to Heaven, and never again abase our sight so low as to permit even one glance at the ground."

The Duke of Gloucester said, using his wife's nickname, "Nell, sweet Nell, if you love your lord, banish the cancer of ambitious thoughts. May that thought, if I should imagine ill against my King and nephew, virtuous Henry VI, result in my last breath in this mortal world! My troubling dream last night makes me sad."

"What did my lord dream? Tell me, and I'll repay you with the sweet recounting of my morning's dream," she said.

In this culture, people believed that morning dreams were true dreams.

The Duke of Gloucester said, "I thought that this staff, my symbol of office at the court, was broken in two; by whom I have forgotten, but I think it was broken by Cardinal Beaufort, and on the pieces of the broken staff were placed the heads of Duke Edmund of Somerset and William de la Pole, who is the first Duke of Suffolk.

"This was my dream. What it forebodes, God knows."

"Tut, this was nothing but an argument that he who breaks a stick of the Duke of Gloucester's grove of trees shall lose his head for his presumption," the Duchess of Gloucester said. "But listen to me, my Humphrey, my sweet Duke.

"I thought I sat in the seat of majesty in the cathedral church of Westminster, and in that chair — the coronation chair — where Kings and Queens are crowned, there Henry VI and Dame Margaret kneeled to me and on my head set the diadem."

"No, Eleanor, then must I chide you outright," the Duke of Gloucester said. "Presumptuous dame, ill-nurtured Eleanor, aren't you the second woman in the realm, second only to the Queen, and aren't you the Lord Protector's wife, and beloved by him? Haven't you worldly pleasure at your command, above and beyond the reach or compass of your thought? And will you still be hammering and working at treachery that will tumble down both your husband and yourself from the top of honor to the feet of disgrace? Get away from me, and let me hear no more about your morning dream!"

"What, what, my lord! Are you so choleric and angry at me, Eleanor, simply because I told you my dream? Next time I'll keep my dreams to myself, and not be rebuked."

The Duke of Gloucester replied, "No, don't be angry; I am pleased again. I am no longer angry."

A messenger entered the room.

The messenger said, "My Lord Protector, it is his highness' pleasure that you prepare to ride to St. Albans, where the King and Queen intend to go hawking."

St. Albans was a town twenty miles north of London.

"I will go," the Duke of Gloucester said, and then added, "Come, Nell, will you ride with us?"

"Yes, my good lord, I'll follow quickly," the Duchess of Gloucester said.

The Duke of Gloucester and the messenger exited.

Alone, the Duchess of Gloucester said to herself, "Follow I must; I cannot go before, while the Duke of Gloucester bears this base and humble mind. If I were a man, a Duke, and the next of blood, I would remove these tedious stumbling blocks and smooth my way upon their headless necks. And, being a woman, I will not be slack to play my part in Lady Fortune's pageant."

She still wanted to be Queen of England.

Sir John Hume, a priest, entered the room. In this culture, priests were called "Sir" as a mark of respect.

Hearing a noise, she said, "Who are you there? Sir John! No, don't be afraid, man. We are alone; here's no one but you and me."

Sir John Hume said, "May Jesus preserve your royal majesty!"

Kings and Queens were called majesty and sometimes grace; Dukes and Duchesses were called only grace.

"What are you saying!" the Duchess of Gloucester said. "Majesty! I am only grace."

"But, by the grace of God, and my advice, your grace's title shall be multiplied," Sir John Hume said.

"What are you saying, man?" she asked. "Have you conferred yet with Margery Jourdain, the cunning witch, and with Roger Bolingbroke, the conjurer who raises spirits? And will they undertake to do me good by helping me to succeed?"

"They have promised to show your highness a spirit raised from the depth of underground — Hell — that shall answer such questions as shall be asked him by your grace."

"It is enough," the Duchess of Gloucester said. "I'll think about the questions I will ask. When we return from St. Albans, we'll see that these things are completely done."

She gave the priest some money and said, "Here, Hume, take this reward; make merry, man, with your confederates in this weighty, important cause."

She exited.

Alone, Sir John Hume said to himself, "I, Hume, must make merry with the Duchess' gold, and by Mother Mary I shall. But be careful now, Sir John Hume! Seal up your lips, and speak no words but stay mum. This business requires silent secrecy.

"Dame Eleanor gives me gold to bring the witch. Gold cannot come amiss, even if the witch were a Devil. Yet I have gold that comes to me from another source. I dare not say it comes from the rich Cardinal Beaufort and from the great and newly made Duke of Suffolk, yet that is the case.

"To be plain, they, knowing Dame Eleanor's aspiring and ambitious disposition, have hired me to undermine the Duchess of Gloucester and buzz these conjurations in her brain.

"People say, proverbially, 'A crafty knave needs no broker,' that is, no agent, yet I am the Duke of Suffolk's and Cardinal Beaufort's broker. Hume, if you are not careful, you shall go near to calling them both a pair of crafty knaves.

"Well, so it stands; and thus, I fear, at last Hume's — my — knavery will be the Duchess of Gloucester's wreck, and her conviction and condemnation will be her husband Humphrey's fall.

"No matter what happens, I shall have gold from them all."

Three or four petitioners stood in front of the palace in London. One of the petitioners was Peter, an apprentice to an armorer. The petitioners had grievances that they hoped the Lord Protector — the Duke of Gloucester — would redress.

The first petitioner said, "My masters, let's stand close together and quietly. My Lord Protector will come this way by and by, and then we may deliver our supplications that are written with a quill."

The second petitioner said, "By the Virgin Mary, may the Lord protect him, for he's a good man! May Jesus bless him!"

The Duke of Suffolk and Queen Margaret came walking toward them.

Peter said, "Here the Lord Protector comes, I think, and the Queen is with him. I'll be the first to present my petition, I am sure."

"Come back, fool," the second petitioner said. "This man is the Duke of Suffolk, and not my Lord Protector."

Hearing them speak, the Duke of Suffolk asked, "How are you, fellow? Do you have any business with me?"

The first petitioner said, "Please, my lord, pardon me. I mistook you for my Lord Protector."

Queen Margaret looked at the petition he was holding and read out loud, "*To my Lord Protector.*"

She then asked, "Are your supplications to his lordship? Let me see them."

She asked the first petitioner, "What is your petition?"

He replied, "Mine is, if it please your grace, against John Goodman, my lord Cardinal Beaufort's man, for keeping my house, and lands, and wife and all, from me."

"Your wife, too!" the Duke of Suffolk said. "That's some wrong, indeed."

He asked the second petitioner, "What's your petition? What's here!"

He read out loud, "*Against the Duke of Suffolk, for enclosing the commons of Melford.*"

Long Melford was a town in Suffolk. The Duke of Suffolk was being accused of fencing in land intended for the use of all the citizens. By fencing in the land, the Duke of Suffolk was keeping it for his own use.

The Duke of Suffolk said, "What is this, Sir Knave!"

The second petitioner said, "Alas, sir, I am but a poor petitioner who is representing our whole township."

Peter handed over his petition, saying, "This is against my master, Thomas Horner, for saying that the Duke of York was rightful heir to the crown."

"What did you say?" Queen Margaret asked. "Did the Duke of York say that he was rightful heir to the crown?"

Peter replied, "Did the Duke of York say that my master was rightful heir to the crown? No, indeed. My master said that he — the Duke of York — was, and that King Henry VI was an usurper."

The Duke of Suffolk called for a servant and then ordered, "Take this fellow in — arrest him — and send an officer to bring his master here immediately."

He said to Peter, "We'll hear more about this petition of yours in the presence of the King."

The servant exited with Peter.

Queen Margaret said to the petitioners, "And as for you petitioners who love to be protected under the wings of our Lord Protector's grace, begin your suits anew, and sue to him."

She tore up the petition mentioning the Duke of York and ordered, "Away, base cullions! Suffolk, let them go."

The word "cullions," which was an insult, literally meant "testicles."

The petitioners all said, "Come, let's go."

They exited.

Queen Margaret said, "My Lord of Suffolk, tell me, is this the custom, is this the fashion in the court of England? Is this the government of Britain's isle, and is this the royalty of Albion's King?"

Britain has had many names; the oldest known name for it is Albion.

She continued, "Shall King Henry VI always be a pupil under the governance of the surly Duke of Gloucester? Am I a Queen in title and in mode of address, and yet must I be made a subject to a Duke?

"I tell you, de la Pole, my Lord of Suffolk, when in the city of Tours you jousted in honor of my love and stole away the French ladies' hearts, I thought King Henry VI resembled you in courage, courtship, and physical shape."

The word "courtship" meant both "wooing" and "courtly manners."

She continued, "But all his mind is bent to holiness, to number Ave-Maria prayers on his beads. His champions are the prophets and apostles. His weapons are the holy sayings of sacred writ. His study is his jousting yard, and his loves are the bronze statues of canonized saints.

"I wish the College of the Cardinals would choose him to be Pope, and carry him away to Rome, and set the triple crown of the Pope upon his head. That would be a position fit for his holiness."

The Pope wears a triple tiara, a crown with three circlets.

The Duke of Suffolk said, "Madam, be calm. As I was the cause of your highness coming to England, so I will work to make your grace fully content in England."

She replied, "Besides the haughty Lord Protector, we have Cardinal Beaufort, the imperious churchman; Somerset, Buckingham, and grumbling York, and even the least of these can do more in England than the King can."

The Duke of Suffolk said, "And he of these who can do most of all cannot do more in England than can the Nevilles: The Earl of Salisbury and the Earl of Warwick are no simple, ordinary, common peers."

Queen Margaret said, "None of these lords vexes me half as much as that proud dame, the Lord Protector's wife, the Duchess of Gloucester. She struts through the court with troops of ladies, more like an empress than Duke Humphrey of Gloucester's wife.

"Foreigners in the court mistake her for the Queen. She wears clothing worth a Duke's revenues on her back, and in her heart she scorns our poverty. Shall I not live to be avenged on her? She is contemptuous — of me! Base-born callet — whore! — that she is, she boasted among her minions the other day that just the train of the worst gown she wears was worth more than all of my father's lands until you, Duke of Suffolk, gave two Dukedoms — Anjou and Maine — in exchange for his daughter."

The Duke of Suffolk replied, "Madam, I myself have limed a bush for her, and placed a choir of such enticing birds, that she will alight to listen to their lays, and never mount to trouble you again."

He was saying that he had set a trap for the Duchess of Gloucester. Birdlime was a sticky substance used to catch birds, and "enticing birds" were decoys. Literally, the "lays" of the birds were their songs. Metaphorically, the lays were words that would be spoken to the Duchess of Gloucester by the witch and conjuror she had hired.

The Duke of Suffolk continued, "So, let her rest, don't worry about her, and madam, listen to me, for I am bold enough to give you counsel in this business.

"Although we don't like Cardinal Beaufort, yet we must join with him and with the lords until we have brought Duke Humphrey of Gloucester into disgrace. As for the Duke of York, this recent complaint made by the petitioner Peter will do little for the Duke's benefit.

"So, one by one, we'll weed them all at last, and you yourself shall steer the happy helm of state."

A trumpet sounded, and several people walked over to the Duke of Suffolk and Queen Margaret. They were King Henry VI, the Duke of Gloucester, the Duke of Buckingham, the Duke of York, the Duke of Somerset, the Earl of Salisbury, the Earl of Warwick, and the Duchess of Gloucester. The Duke of York and the Duke of Somerset were on either side of the King, whispering to him and trying to influence him.

The Duke of Somerset was wearing a red rose, the emblem of the Lancastrians.

The Duke of York and the Earl of Warwick were each wearing a white rose.

King Henry VI said, "For my part, noble lords, I don't care which person becomes Regent of France: Somerset or York. It's all the same to me."

The Duke of York said, "If I have badly behaved in France, then let me be denied the Regentship."

The Duke of Somerset said, "If I am unworthy of the position, then let the Duke of York be Regent; I will yield the position to him."

The Earl of Warwick said to the Duke of Somerset, "Don't argue about whether your grace is worthy, yes or no. The Duke of York is worthier to become Regent of France."

Cardinal Beaufort said, "Ambitious Warwick, let your betters speak."

The Earl of Warwick replied, "Cardinal Beaufort is not my better in the battlefield."

The Duke of Buckingham said, "All present are your betters, Warwick."

"Warwick may live to be the best of all," the Earl of Warwick replied, referring to himself in the third person.

"Peace, son!" the Earl of Salisbury said to the Earl of Warwick. He added, "And give us some reasons, Buckingham, why Somerset should be preferred in this."

Queen Margaret interrupted, "Because the King, indeed, will have it so."

Actually, the King had said that he had no preference.

The Duke of Gloucester said, "Madam, the King is old enough himself to give his opinion. These are no matters for women."

"If the King is old enough, why does your grace need to be Protector of his excellence the King?" Queen Margaret asked.

"Madam, I am Protector of the Realm," the Duke of Gloucester said. "And, at the King's pleasure, I will resign my place."

The Duke of Suffolk said, "Resign it then and leave your insolence. Since you have been King — as who is King but you? — the commonwealth has daily run to wrack and ruin, the Dauphin has prevailed beyond the seas, and all the peers and nobles of the realm have been as bondsmen to your sovereignty."

By "the Dauphin," they meant King Charles VII of France. Since the English regarded King Henry VI as the true King of France, they referred to Charles VII as the Dauphin.

The dictionary definition of "dauphin" is "the oldest son of the King of France."

Cardinal Beaufort said, "You have racked the common citizens, torturing them with excessive taxation — it is as if they have been tortured on the rack. The clergy's moneybags are lank and lean and empty as a result of your extortions."

The Duke of Somerset said, "Your sumptuous buildings and your wife's attire have cost a mass of public treasury."

The Duke of Buckingham said, "Your cruelty in execution upon offenders has exceeded the law and left you to the mercy of the law. Your implementation of penalties for breaking the law has been too harsh."

Queen Margaret said, "The sale of official positions and towns in France, if they were known to be true, as the suspicion is great, would make you quickly hop without your head.'

She was threatening the Duke of Gloucester with beheading.

Angry, the Duke of Gloucester left rather than say something that could hurt him. Queen Margaret and her allies had much power.

Queen Margaret deliberately dropped her fan and said to the Duchess of Gloucester, "Give me my fan."

The Duchess of Gloucester was slow to obey, and Queen Margaret said, "Minion, won't you pick up and give me my fan!"

In this context, the word "minion" was derogatory and meant "underling."

Queen Margaret hit the Duchess of Gloucester on the ear and said, "I beg your pardon, madam; was it you I hit?"

"Was it I!" an angry Duchess of Gloucester said. "Yes, it was I, proud Frenchwoman! If I could come near your beauty with my fingernails, I'd set my ten commandments in your face."

God was believed to have written the Ten Commandments on two stone tablets with his fingernails.

King Henry VI said to his aunt, the Duchess of Gloucester, "Sweet aunt, be calm. It was against her will — it was unintentional."

"Against her will!" the Duchess of Gloucester said. "Good King, beware before it's too late. She'll hamper you, and dandle you like a baby. Although in this place the greatest master wears no breeches because she is the Queen and not the King, she shall not strike Dame Eleanor of Gloucester unrevenged."

The Duchess of Gloucester exited.

The Duke of Buckingham said quietly to only the Cardinal, "Lord Cardinal Beaufort, I will follow Dame Eleanor of Gloucester, and look for Duke Humphrey of Gloucester in order to see how he proceeds and conducts himself. Dame Eleanor of Gloucester is ticked off now. Her fury needs no spurs; she'll gallop far enough to her destruction."

The Duke of Buckingham exited as the Duke of Gloucester, now calmer, returned and said, "Lords, now that my anger has blown over while I walked once about the quadrangle, I have come back to talk about the affairs of the commonwealth. As for your spiteful false objections, prove them and I will lie open to the law. But may God in mercy so deal with my soul as I in duty love my King and country! But, to the matter that we have in hand: I say, my sovereign, that the Duke of York is the fittest man to be your Regent in the realm of France."

The Duke of Suffolk said, "Before we make the choice of who is to be Regent of France, give me permission to show some evidence, of no little force, that the Duke of York is the most unfitting of any man."

The Duke of York said, "I'll tell you, Duke of Suffolk, why I am unfitting. First, because I cannot flatter you and still keep my pride, Next, if I am appointed as the Regent in France, my Lord of Somerset will keep me here, without payment, money, or military equipment, until France has been won by the French and placed into the Dauphin's hands. The last time I danced attendance on the Duke of Somerset's will, I was kept waiting until Paris was besieged, famished, and lost."

The Earl of Warwick said, "That I can bear witness to, and no traitor has ever in the land committed a fouler deed."

Actually, both the Duke of York and the Duke of Somerset had been at fault for not coming to the aid of the English military leader Lord Talbot, who died as a result of their inaction. The death of Lord Talbot led to many French victories.

"Peace, headstrong Warwick!" the Duke of Suffolk said. "Be quiet!"

"Image of pride, why should I hold my peace?" the Earl of Warwick replied.

Guards brought in Horner the armorer and Peter, his apprentice.

The Duke of Suffolk replied to the Earl of Warwick, "Because here is a man accused of treason. Pray to God that the Duke of York is able to excuse himself!"

The Duke of York asked, "Does anyone accuse me of being a traitor?"

King Henry VI asked, "What do you mean, Duke of Suffolk? Tell me, who are these men?"

The Duke of Suffolk replied, "If it pleases your majesty, this is the man who is accusing his master of high treason. He said that Richard, Duke of York, was the rightful heir to the English crown and that your majesty was a usurper."

"Tell me, man, were these your words?" King Henry VI asked Horner.

He replied, "If it shall please your majesty, I never said or thought any such thing. God is my witness: I am falsely accused by this villain."

Peter said, holding up his ten fingers, "By these ten bones, my lords, he did speak them to me in the garret one night, as we were scouring my Lord of York's armor."

The Duke of York said to Horner, "Base dunghill villain and craftsman! I'll have your head for this traitorous speech of yours."

He then said to King Henry VI, "I beseech your royal majesty to let him have all the rigor of the law."

Horner said, "Alas, my lord, hang me, if I ever spoke those words. My accuser is Peter, my apprentice, and when I punished him for his mistake the other day, he vowed upon his knees that he would get even with me. I have good witness and evidence for this; therefore, I beseech your majesty to not cast away an honest man because of a villain's accusation."

King Henry VI asked the Duke of Gloucester, "Uncle, what shall we say to this in law?"

The Duke of Gloucester said, "This is my decision, if I may judge. Let the Duke of Somerset be the Regent over the French, because this accusation breeds suspicion against the Duke of York, and let these two men — Horner and Peter — have a day appointed for them to fight a single combat in a convenient place because Horner has witness and evidence of his servant's malice. This is the law, and this is Duke Humphrey's judgment."

Peter had made an accusation against Horner, who had defended himself by giving a reason for why Peter could be lying. To decide the matter, since it could not be decided on the basis of the evidence available, the two would fight a single combat. This culture believed that God would help the person in the right to defeat the person in the wrong, and so the victor of the single combat would be in the right.

"I humbly thank your royal majesty," the Duke of Somerset said to King Henry VI.

He addressed his thanks to the King rather than to the Duke of Gloucester because the Duke of Gloucester had made the decision on behalf of the King.

Horner said, "And I accept the combat willingly."

"Alas, my lord, I cannot fight," Peter said. "For God's sake, pity my case. The spite of man prevails against me. Oh, Lord, have mercy upon me! I shall never be able to fight a blow. Oh, Lord, my heart!"

"Sirrah, either you must fight, or else you must be hanged," the Duke of Gloucester said to Peter.

"Take them away to prison," King Henry VI said, "and the day of combat shall be the last day of the next month.

"Come, Duke of Somerset, we'll see you sent on your way."

Margery Jourdain the witch, Sir John Hume and Sir John Southwell the priests, and Roger Bolingbroke the conjuror met in the Duke of Gloucester's garden.

Sir John Hume said, "Come, my masters; the Duchess of Gloucester, I tell you, expects performance of your promises."

"Master Hume, we are therefore prepared," Roger Bolingbroke the conjuror said. "Will her ladyship behold and hear our conjurations?"

"Yes, what else? Of course she will," Sir John Hume said. "Don't be afraid that she lacks courage."

Roger Bolingbroke the conjuror said, "I have heard her reported to be a woman of an invincible spirit, but it shall be convenient, Master Hume, that you be near her on a higher place, while we are busy below; and so, please go, in God's name, and leave us."

Sir John Hume exited.

Roger Bolingbroke the conjuror added, "Mother Jourdain, lie prostrate and grovel on the earth. John Southwell, you read the conjuration, and let us go to our work."

The Duchess of York and Sir John Hume appeared at a higher spot, and the Duchess, who had heard Bolingbroke's most recent words, said, "Well said, my masters; and welcome, all of you. Let's attend to this business, the sooner the better."

"Have patience, good lady," Roger Bolingbroke the conjuror said. "Wizards know their times. Deep night, dark night, the silent part of the night, the time of night when the city of Troy was set on fire and sacked by the Greeks, the time when screech owls cry and chained guard dogs howl, and spirits walk and ghosts break out of their graves, that time best fits the work we have in hand. Madam, sit and don't be afraid. That spirit we raise, we will make fast within a hallowed verge — a sacred circle."

They performed the relevant ceremonies and made the circle. Southwell read from the conjuring book the spell beginning "*Conjuro te*," which is Latin for "I conjure you."

As thunder sounded and lightning flashed, a spirit arose and said, "*Adsum*."

"*Adsum*" is Latin for "I am present."

Margery Jourdain the witch said, "Asnath, by the eternal God, whose name and power you tremble at, answer what I shall ask because until you speak, you shall not pass from hence."

"Asnath" was an anagram form for "Sathan," which is a form of the name "Satan."

The spirit replied, "Ask what thou wilt. I wish that I had already finished answering your questions!"

The questions to be asked were already written down. Roger Bolingbroke the conjuror read, "*First about the King: What shall become of him?*"

The spirit replied, "The Duke yet lives whom Henry shall depose, but him outlive and die a violent death."

Like many such answers, this answer was equivocal. Would the Duke depose Henry, or would Henry depose the Duke? Would Henry outlive the Duke and die a violent death, or would the Duke outlive Henry and die a violent death?

Southwell wrote down the answer.

Roger Bolingbroke the conjuror read, "*What fates await the Duke of Suffolk?*"

The spirit replied, "By water shall he die, and take his end."

Again, this answer was ambiguous. "He shall die by water" can mean 1) "He shall drown," or 2) "He shall die on a seashore." Or as will be seen, it could also have a much different meaning.

Roger Bolingbroke the conjuror read, "*What shall befall the Duke of Somerset?*"

The spirit replied, "Let him shun castles. Safer shall he be upon the sandy plains than where castles mounted stand. Have done, for more I hardly can endure."

Again, this answer was ambiguous. It could mean, "Let him shun castles mounted high on mountains." Or as will be seen, it could also have a much different meaning.

Roger Bolingbroke the conjuror said to the spirit, "Descend to darkness and the burning lake! False fiend, leave!"

Thunder sounded and lightning flashed as the spirit exited.

The Duke of York and the Duke of Buckingham broke into the garden with their guards.

The Duke of York said, "Lay hands upon these traitors and their trash — their conjuring materials."

He said to Margery Jourdain the witch, "Beldam, I think we watched you closely."

He then pretended to be surprised to see the Duchess of Gloucester and said sarcastically, "Madam, is that you there? The King and the commonwealth are deeply indebted to you for this piece of labor. My Lord Protector will, I don't doubt, see you well rewarded for these good deserts."

The Duchess of Gloucester replied, "These good deserts are not half as bad as yours to England's King, you insulting Duke who threatens where there's no reason to threaten."

The Duke of Buckingham said sarcastically, "True, madam, no reason at all." He then pointed at the conjuring materials and said, "What do you call this?

"Away with them! Let them be securely imprisoned and kept apart from one another.

"You, madam, shall come with us.

"Stafford, arrest her."

Stafford and some guards took away the Duchess of Gloucester and Sir John Hume.

The Duke of Buckingham said, "We'll see to it that your conjuring materials here will all be produced as evidence in a court of law.

"Take them away!"

Some guards took away Margery Jourdain the witch, Roger Bolingbroke the conjuror, and Sir John Southwell.

The Duke of York said, "Lord Buckingham, I think that you watched her well. This is a pretty plot, well chosen to build upon! Now, please, my lord, let's see the Devil's writ. What have we here?"

He read out loud, "*The Duke yet lives whom Henry shall depose, but him outlive and die a violent death*."

He said, "This is just '*Aio te, Aeacida, Romanos vincere posse*.'"

Pyrrhus had asked an oracle whether he could conquer Rome, and the oracle had answered with the Latin prophecy that the Duke of York had quoted. Like many prophecies, the oracle's prophecy was ambiguous: "I prophesy that you, the descendant of Aeacus, the Romans to conquer are able."

This could mean, "I prophesy that you, the descendant of Aeacus, are able to conquer the Romans" or "I prophesy that the Romans are able to conquer you, the descendant of Aeacus."

The Duke of York then read out loud, "*Tell me what fate awaits the Duke of Suffolk? By water shall he die, and take his end. What shall betide the Duke of Somerset? Let him shun castles; safer shall he be upon the sandy plains than where castles mounted stand.*"

He then said, "Come, come, my lords; these oracles are hardily attained, and hardily understood. It is difficult to receive an oracle, and it is difficult to understand the oracle once it is received.

"The King is now progressing towards St. Albans. With him goes the husband of this lovely lady, the Duchess of Gloucester. Thither take this news as fast as horse can carry it. This news will be a sorry breakfast for my Lord Protector."

The Duke of Buckingham said, "Your grace shall give me permission, my Lord of York, to be the post and carry the message, in hope of being rewarded by King Henry VI."

"At your pleasure, my good lord," the Duke of York replied. "Yes, you shall carry this news to the King."

He then called for a servant, "Who's within there, ho!"

A servingman entered.

The Duke of York ordered him, "Invite my Lords of Salisbury and Warwick to dine with me tomorrow night.

"Let's go!"

Being a witch or wizard and engaging in witchcraft and sorcery were serious offenses, especially since King Henry VI was very religious. Here are a few Bible verses (King James Version) about witches:

Leviticus 19:31: *Regard not them that have familiar spirits, neither seek after wizards, to be defiled by them: I am the LORD your God.*

Exodus 22:18: *Thou shalt not suffer a witch to live.*

Leviticus 20:27: *A man also or woman that hath a familiar spirit, or that is a wizard, shall surely be put to death: they shall stone them with stones: their blood shall be upon them.*

Deuteronomy 18:10-11: *There shall not be found among you any one that maketh his son or his daughter to pass through the fire, or that useth divination, or an observer of times, or an enchanter, or a witch, / Or a charmer, or a consulter with familiar spirits, or a wizard, or a necromancer.*

Leviticus 20:6: *And the soul that turneth after such as have familiar spirits, and after wizards, to go a whoring after them, I will even set my face against that soul, and will cut him off from among his people.*

A familiar is a witch's attending spirit; often it has the form of an animal.

CHAPTER 2

— 2.1 —

Several people were hunting with hawks at St. Albans: King Henry VI, Queen Margaret, the Duke of Gloucester, Cardinal Beaufort, and the Duke of Suffolk. Some other falconers were hallowing to encourage the dogs to force the waterfowl into the air where hawks could seize them.

Queen Margaret said, "Believe me, lords, for hunting with hawks at the brook, I have not seen better entertainment for the past seven years. Yet, by your leave, the wind was very high, and I would have bet ten to one that old Joan the hawk would not have gone out and hunted."

On very windy days, hawks were not used in hunting.

King Henry VI said to the Duke of Gloucester, "But what a point — position for attacking — your falcon made, my lord, and what a height she flew above the rest! To see how God in all his creatures works! Yes, Mankind and birds are eager to climb high."

The Duke of Suffolk said, "It is no marvel, if it pleases your majesty, that my Lord Protector's hawks tower and soar so well. They know their master loves to be aloft and bears his thoughts above his falcon's pitch."

The word "pitch" means the greatest height a hawk will climb before swooping.

The Duke of Gloucester said, "My lord, it is but a base and ignoble mind that mounts no higher than a bird can soar."

Cardinal Beaufort said, "I thought as much; the Duke of Gloucester wants to be above the clouds."

The Duke of Gloucester asked, "My lord Cardinal, what do you mean by that? Wouldn't it be good if your grace could fly to Heaven?"

King Henry VI said, "Heaven is the treasury of everlasting joy."

Cardinal Beaufort said to the Duke of Gloucester, "Your Heaven is on Earth. Your eyes and thoughts are obsessed with a crown, which is the treasure of your heart, pernicious Protector, dangerous peer, who so flatters the King and commonwealth!"

Matthew 6:19-21 (King James Version) states this:

19 *Lay not up for yourselves treasures upon earth, where moth and rust doth corrupt, and where thieves break through and steal:*

20 *But lay up for yourselves treasures in Heaven, where neither moth nor rust doth corrupt, and where thieves do not break through nor steal:*

21 *For where your treasure is, there will your heart be also.*

The Duke of Gloucester replied, "Cardinal Beaufort, have you as a priest grown imperious and dictatorial? '*Tantaene animis coelestibus irae?*' Are churchmen so hot? Good uncle, hide such malice. With all of your 'holiness,' can you do it?"

"*Tantaene animis coelestibus irae?*" is a Latin quotation from Virgil's *Aeneid* 1:11. Translated, it means, "Is there such anger in the minds of Heavenly beings?"

Cardinal Beaufort and the Duke of Gloucester were related. The Duke of Gloucester's father was King Henry IV. Cardinal Beaufort was King Henry IV's half-brother. When Cardinal Beaufort was born, his parents were not married, but they married afterward. John of Gaunt is Cardinal Beaufort's father and the Duke of Gloucester's grandfather.

The Duke of Suffolk said, "There is no malice, sir — no more than well becomes so good a quarrel and so bad a peer."

"So bad a peer as whom, my lord?" the Duke of Gloucester asked.

"Why, as you, my lord," the Duke of Suffolk said, "if it pleases your lordly Lord Protectorship."

"Why, Suffolk, England knows your insolence," the Duke of Gloucester said.

"And it knows your ambition, Gloucester," Queen Margaret said.

"Please, be calm and peaceful, good Queen," King Henry VI said, "and don't incite these furious peers, for blessed are the peacemakers on earth."

Cardinal Beaufort said, "Let me be blessed for the peace I make, against this proud Lord Protector, with my sword!"

The Duke of Gloucester said quietly so that only Cardinal Beaufort could hear him, "Indeed, holy uncle, I wish that it would come to that — an armed single combat between us two!"

Cardinal Beaufort whispered to the Duke of Gloucester, "By the Virgin Mary, I am ready whenever you dare to fight me."

The Duke of Gloucester whispered to Cardinal Beaufort, "Don't gather supporters to back you in a fight. You yourself shall pay for your insults."

Cardinal Beaufort whispered to the Duke of Gloucester, "Yes, I shall pay where you dare not peep. If you dare to fight me, let's fight this evening, on the east side of the grove."

"What's going on, my lords?" King Henry VI asked them.

Cardinal Beaufort said out loud, "Believe me, cousin Gloucester, if your servant had not caused the fowl to rise from cover so suddenly, we would have had more sport."

He was pretending to have been talking to the Duke of Gloucester only about hawking.

He then whispered to the Duke of Gloucester, "Come with your two-handed sword — your long sword."

"I truly will, uncle," the Duke of Gloucester replied.

Cardinal Beaufort whispered to the Duke of Gloucester, "Do you agree? The east side of the grove?"

The Duke of Gloucester whispered, "Cardinal, I will fight you there."

"Why, what's going on, uncle Gloucester!" King Henry VI asked.

"We are talking about hawking — nothing else, my lord," the Duke of Gloucester replied.

He whispered to Cardinal Beaufort, "Now, by God's mother, priest, I'll shave your crown for this, or all my skill in fencing shall fail."

Cardinal Beaufort whispered to the Duke of Gloucester, "*Medice, teipsum.* Protector, see to it well — protect yourself."

Luke 4:23 in the Vulgate Bible stated in part, "*Medice, cura teipsum.*" *Teipsum* can be written *te ipsum*. The Latin meant, "Physician, cure yourself." The words had become proverbial and the Latin word "*cura*" was understood.

King Henry VI said, "The winds grow high; so does your anger, lords. How irksome is this music to my heart! When such strings jar, what hope do we have of harmony? Please, my lords, let me settle this strife."

A townsman of St. Albans arrived, crying, "A miracle!"

The Duke of Gloucester asked, "What is the meaning of this noise? Fellow, what miracle are you proclaiming?"

"A miracle! A miracle!" the townsman cried.

The Duke of Suffolk said, "Come to the King and tell him what miracle."

"Truly, within this past half-hour a blind man at St. Albans' shrine that is devoted to St. Alban has received his sight. He is a man who was born blind and never saw in his life before."

St. Albans was named after St. Alban, the first British saint.

King Henry VI said, "Now, God be praised, Who to believing souls gives light in darkness, and comfort in despair!"

The Mayor of St. Albans and some townsmen arrived. Some townsmen were carrying Simpcox in a chair. Simpcox' wife followed behind the others.

Cardinal Beaufort said, "Here come the townsmen in a procession to show the man to your highness."

"Great is his comfort in this earthly vale, although by his sight his sin will be multiplied," King Henry VI said.

He meant that the gift of sight would increase the man's temptations to sin.

"Stand by, my masters," the Duke of Gloucester said. "Bring him near the King. His highness' pleasure is to talk with him."

"Good fellow, tell us here the circumstances of your receiving sight, so that we for you may glorify the Lord," King Henry VI said. "Have you been blind a long time and is your sight now restored?"

"I was born blind, if it pleases your grace," Simpcox said.

"Yes, indeed, he was," his wife said.

"What woman is this?" the Duke of Suffolk asked.

"I am his wife, if it pleases your worship," she replied.

The Duke of Gloucester, already suspicious of the miracle, said, "If you had been his mother, you would have been in a better position to say that."

"Where were you born?" King Henry VI asked.

"At Berwick in the north, if it pleases your grace," Simpcox replied.

Berwick is located near the Scottish border.

"Poor soul, God's goodness has been great to you," King Henry VI said. "Never let a day or a night pass without saying your prayers, but always remember what the Lord has done for you."

"Tell me, good fellow," Queen Margaret said, "did you come here to this holy shrine by chance, or out of devotion?"

"God knows that I came out of pure devotion," Simpcox said. "I was called to come here a hundred times and oftener in my sleep by good St. Alban, who said, 'Simpcox, come, come, make an offering at my shrine, and I will help you.'"

Simpcox' wife said, "This is very true, indeed; and many time and often I myself have heard a voice call to him so."

Because Simpcox had been carried in a chair, Cardinal Beaufort asked, "Are you lame?"

"Yes, may God Almighty help me!" Simpcox replied.

"How did you come to be lame?" the Duke of Suffolk asked.

"I fell out of a tree," Simpcox replied.

His wife added, "A plum tree, master."

The Duke of Gloucester asked, "How long have you been blind?"

"I was born blind, master," Simpcox replied.

"Born blind, and yet you climbed a tree?" the Duke of Gloucester asked.

"Just once in all my life, when I was a youth," Simpcox replied.

"That is too true, and his climbing cost him very dear," his wife said.

"By the Mass, you must have really loved plums, if you would risk climbing a tree to get them," the Duke of Gloucester said.

"Alas, good master, my wife desired some damsons, and made me climb to get them, despite the danger to my life," Simpcox said.

Some bawdy humor was being expressed here. "Plum tree" was slang for a woman's crotch and thighs. "Climbing a plum tree" was slang for mounting and having sex with a woman. "Damsons" was a word that meant 1) a kind of small plum and 2) testicles.

The Duke of Gloucester thought to himself, *He is a cunning knave, but he won't get away with this.*

He said out loud to Simpcox, "Let me see your eyes. Close them; now open them. In my opinion you still do not see well."

"Yes, I do, master," Simpcox said. "I see as clear as day, for which I thank God and St. Alban."

"Tell me," the Duke of Gloucester said, "what color is this cloak?"

"It is red, master; it is as red as blood," Simpcox replied.

"Why, that's well said. What color is my gown?" the Duke of Gloucester asked.

"It is black, indeed," Simpcox said. "It is as black as coal; it is as black as jet."

Jet is a kind of black coal.

Suddenly suspicious, King Henry VI asked, "How do you know what color jet is?"

"I think he has never seen jet," the Duke of Suffolk said.

The Duke of Gloucester said, "But he has seen many cloaks and gowns before this day."

Simpcox' wife said, "Before today, he has never seen any cloaks and gowns."

The Duke of Gloucester asked, "Tell me, sirrah, what's my name?"

Simpcox replied, "Alas, master, I don't know your name."

The Duke of Gloucester pointed to a man and asked, "What's his name?"

"I don't know," Simpcox said.

The Duke of Gloucester pointed to another man and asked, "Do you know his name?"

"No, indeed, master."

"What's your own name?"

"Saunder Simpcox, if it pleases you, master."

"Then, Saunder, sit there," the Duke of Gloucester said. "You are the lyingest knave in Christendom. If you had been born blind, you might as well have known all our names as thus to name the several colors we wear. Sight may distinguish among colors, but for a just-sighted person to immediately be able to name them all is impossible.

"My lords, St. Alban here has done a miracle, and wouldn't you think the cunning to be great of any person who could restore this cripple to his legs again?"

"Oh, master, I wish that you could!" Simpcox said.

The Duke of Gloucester asked, "My masters of St. Albans, don't you have beadles — parish officers — in your town, and things called whips?"

The Mayor of St. Albans replied, "Yes, my lord, if it pleases your grace."

"Then send for one of each immediately," the Duke of Gloucester said.

The Mayor ordered an attendant, "Sirrah, go fetch the beadle and his whip here straightaway."

An attendant exited to carry out the order.

The Duke of Gloucester said, "Now fetch for me a stool here immediately."

He then said to Simpcox, "Now, sirrah, if you mean to save yourself from a whipping, leap over this stool and run away."

"Alas, master, I am not able to stand by myself," Simpcox said. "You are about to torture me in vain."

A beadle arrived, carrying a whip.

The Duke of Gloucester said, "Well, sir, we must have you find your legs.

"Sirrah beadle, whip him until he leaps over that stool."

The beadle replied, "I will, my lord."

He then said to Simpcox, "Come on, sirrah; take your jacket off quickly."

"Alas, master, what shall I do?" Simpcox asked. "I am not able to stand."

The beadle hit Simpcox once with the whip, and Simpcox leapt over the stool and ran away. Some townsmen ran after him and cried, "A miracle!"

King Henry VI said, "Oh, God, can You see this, and tolerate it for so long?"

Queen Margaret said, "It made me laugh to see the villain run."

The Duke of Gloucester ordered, "Follow the knave; and take this drab — Simpcox' slut — away."

Simpcox' wife said, "Alas, sir, we did it out of pure need."

They had been hoping that the King would give them money.

The Duke of Gloucester ordered, "Let them be whipped through every market town until they come to the town of Berwick, from whence they came."

Simpcox' wife, the beadle, the Mayor, and the townspeople exited.

Cardinal Beaufort said, "Duke Humphrey of Gloucester has done a miracle today."

"That is true," the Duke of Suffolk said. "He made the lame leap and flee away."

The Duke of Gloucester said, "But you have done more miracles than I: You made in a day, my lord, whole towns flee away."

He was referring to the giving away of Anjou and Maine, and these regions' towns, in exchange for Margaret.

The Duke of Buckingham arrived.

King Henry VI asked, "What tidings come with our kinsman Buckingham? What news do you have?"

The Duke of Buckingham replied, "My news is such that my heart trembles to reveal. A gang of wicked persons, evilly inclined, under the approval and collusion of Lady Eleanor, the Lord Protector's wife, who is the ringleader and head of all this evil company, has conspired dangerously against your state. They have been dealing with witches and with conjurers whom we have apprehended in the act of raising up wicked spirits from underground and asking them about

King Henry VI's life and death, and the life and death of other members of your highness' Privy Council, as in full detail your grace shall understand."

Cardinal Beaufort whispered to the Duke of Gloucester, "And so, my Lord Protector, by this means your lady — your wife — is awaiting trial at London. This news, I think, has blunted your weapon's edge; it is likely, my lord, you will not keep your appointment you made with me to fight a duel."

The Duke of Gloucester replied, "Ambitious churchman, stop afflicting my heart. Sorrow and grief have vanquished all my powers, and vanquished as I am, I yield to you, or to the lowest servant."

"Oh, God, what evils work the wicked ones, heaping confusion on their own heads thereby!" King Henry VI said.

Queen Margaret said, "Gloucester, see here the defilement of your nest. It is best for you to make sure that you are faultless."

The Duke of Gloucester replied, "Madam, as for myself, I call on Heaven to corroborate how I have loved my King and commonwealth. And, as for my wife, I don't know what the facts are, but I am sorry to hear what I have heard just now. Noble she is, but if she has forgotten honor and virtue and conversed with such people as, similar to pitch, defile nobility, I banish her from my bed and company and I give her as a prey to law and shame — to them I give this woman who has dishonored Gloucester's honest name."

King Henry VI said, "Well, for this night we will repose here. Tomorrow we will head back toward London again, to look into this business thoroughly and call these foul offenders to their interrogation and weigh the case in justice's scales. The scales of justice are equal, and the scales' beam stands sure, certain, and reliable. We will find out whose rightful cause prevails. We will discover the truth."

The Duke of York, the Earl of Salisbury, and the Earl of Warwick talked together in the Duke of York's garden.

The Duke of York said, "Now, my good Lords of Salisbury and Warwick, our simple supper ended, give me permission in this private footpath to satisfy myself. I want to know your opinion of my title and right — which are infallible — to England's crown."

The Earl of Salisbury said, "My lord, I long to hear in full about your claim to the crown."

"Sweet York, begin," the Earl of Warwick said, "and if your claim to the crown is good, the Nevilles — both I and my father, the Earl of Salisbury — are your subjects to command."

The Duke of York said, "Then I will begin.

"King Edward III, my lords, had seven sons.

"The first son was Edward the Black Prince, Prince of Wales.

"The second son was William of Hatfield, who was born 16 February 1337 and died 8 July 1337.

"The third son was Lionel, Duke of Clarence.

"The fourth son was John of Gaunt, Duke of Lancaster.

"The fifth son was Edmund Langley, Duke of York.

"The sixth son was Thomas of Woodstock, Duke of Gloucester.

"The seventh and last son was William of Windsor, who was born 24 June 1348 and died 5 September 1348.

"Edward the Black Prince died before his father and left behind him King Richard II, his only son, who after Edward III's death reigned as King until Henry Bolingbroke, Duke of Lancaster, who was the eldest son and heir of John of Gaunt, was crowned by the name of King Henry IV.

"Henry Bolingbroke seized the realm, deposed the rightful King Richard II, sent Richard II's poor Queen to France, from whence she came, and sent Richard II to Pomfret, where, as you know, harmless Richard II was murdered traitorously."

The Earl of Warwick said, "Father, the Duke of York has told the truth. This is how the House of Lancaster got the crown."

The Duke of York said, "And now the House of Lancaster holds the crown by force and not by right.

"Once Richard II, the first son's heir, was dead, the issue — one of the children — of the next son of Edward III should have reigned."

The Earl of Salisbury said, "The second son was William of Hatfield, and he died without an heir."

The Duke of York said, "The third son, Duke Lionel of Clarence, from whose line I claim the crown, had issue: Philippa, a daughter, who married Edmund Mortimer, fourth Earl of March.

"Edmund had issue: Roger, fifth Earl of March.

"And Roger had issue: Edmund, Anne, and Eleanor."

The Earl of Salisbury said, "This last Edmund, in the reign of Henry Bolingbroke as Henry IV, as I have read, laid claim to the crown. Edmund would have been King, but Owen Glendower kept Edmund in captivity until he died.

"But tell us the rest of what you have to say."

The Duke of York said, "Edmund's eldest sister, Anne, who is my mother, being heir to the crown married Richard, the Earl of Cambridge, who was the son of Edmund Langley, King Edward III's fifth son.

"By Anne I claim the Kingdom of England. She was heir to Roger, the Earl of March, who was the son of Edmund Mortimer, who married Philippa, the only daughter of Lionel, the Duke of Clarence.

"So, if the issue of the elder son succeeds to the throne before the issue of the younger son, I am the true and rightful King of England."

The Earl of Warwick said, "What plain proceeding — line of descent — is plainer than this?

"Henry VI claims the crown from John of Gaunt, the fourth son of Edward III.

"The Duke of York claims it from the third son of Edward III."

True, but the Duke of York's claim to the throne was in part from the female line: his mother: Edmund's eldest sister, Anne, who was his mother.

Henry VI's claim to the throne was through the male line: John of Gaunt, then Henry IV, and then Henry V.

The Earl of Warwick continued, "What Until Duke Lionel of Clarence's line fails, the issue of John of Gaunt should not reign.

"Duke Lionel of Clarence's line has not yet failed, for it flourishes in you, the Duke of York, and in your sons, who are the fair slips of such a stock — branches of the trunk of the family tree.

"So then, father Salisbury, let us kneel together; and in this private plot we will be the first who shall salute our rightful sovereign and acknowledge the honor of his birthright to the crown."

The Earl of Salisbury and the Earl of Warwick knelt and said, "Long live our sovereign Richard, who is both the Duke of York and England's King!"

Using the royal plural, the Duke of York said, "We thank you, lords."

He then said, "But I am not officially your King until I am crowned and my sword is stained with the heart-blood of the House of Lancaster; and that's not to be performed immediately, but with deliberation and silent secrecy.

"Both of you must do what I do in these dangerous days.

"Shut your eyes and pretend not to notice the Duke of Suffolk's insolence and arrogance, Cardinal Beaufort's pride, the Duke of Somerset's ambition. Shut your eyes and pretend not to notice the Duke of Buckingham and all the rest of the crew of them until they have snared the shepherd of the flock, that virtuous Prince, the good Humphrey, Duke of Gloucester. He is whom they seek to snare and destroy, and they in seeking that shall find their deaths, if the Duke of York can prophesy."

The Earl of Salisbury said, "My lord, you need say no more; we know your mind at full — we know what you mean to do."

The Earl of Warwick said, "My heart assures me that the Earl of Warwick shall one day make the Duke of York a King."

The Duke of York replied, "And, Neville, this I assure myself: Richard, Duke of York, shall live to make the Earl of Warwick the greatest man in England except for the King."

<h1 style="text-align:center">— 2.3 —</h1>

In a hall of justice, the trial of Eleanor, Duchess of Gloucester, was taking place. Present were King Henry VI, Queen Margaret, the Duke of Gloucester, the Duke of York, the Duke of Suffolk, and the Earl of Salisbury. Also present were the defendants — the Duchess of Gloucester, Margaret Jourdain the witch, John Southwell and John Hume the priests, and Roger Bolingbroke the conjuror — all of whom were under guard and all of whom had been found guilty. Now they were learning what their punishment would be.

King Henry VI said, "Stand forth, Dame Eleanor Cobham, wife of the Duke of Gloucester. In the sight of God and us, your guilt is great. Receive the sentence of the law for sins such as by God's book are punished by death."

Exodus 22:18 states, "*Thou shalt not suffer a witch to live*" (King James Version).

King Henry VI continued, speaking to Margaret Jourdain the witch, John Southwell and John Hume the priests, and Roger Bolingbroke the conjuror, "You four shall go from here back again to prison, and from there to the place of execution. The witch in Smithfield shall be burned to ashes, and you three shall be strangled — hung — on the gallows."

He then said to the Duchess of York, "You, madam, because you are more nobly born, will be dispossessed of your honor in your life, and you shall, after three days of open penance have been done, live in your country here in banishment, with Sir John Stanley, in the Isle of Man."

The Duchess of Gloucester replied, "Welcome is banishment; also welcome would be my death."

The Duke of Gloucester said to her, "Eleanor, the law, you see, has judged you. I cannot excuse and exonerate a person whom the law condemns."

The Duchess of Gloucester and the other prisoners, under guard, exited.

Humphrey, Duke of Gloucester, said, "My eyes are full of tears, and my heart is full of grief. Ah, Humphrey, this dishonor in your old age will bring your head with sorrow to the ground! I ask your majesty to give me permission to go. Sorrow needs solace, and my old age needs ease."

"Wait, Humphrey, Duke of Gloucester," King Henry VI said. "Before you go, give up your staff of office. I, Henry VI, will to myself be my own Lord

Protector, and God shall be my hope, my stay and support, my guide, and my lantern to my feet."

Psalm 71:5 states, "*For thou art my hope, O Lord God* [...]" (King James Version).

Psalm 18:19 states, "*They prevented me in the day of my calamity: but the Lord was my stay*" (King James Version).

Isaiah 58:11 states, "*And the Lord shall guide thee continually, and satisfy thy soul in drought, and make fat thy bones: and thou shalt be like a watered garden, and like a spring of water, whose waters fail not*" (King James Version).

Psalm 119:105 states, "*Thy word is a lamp unto my feet, and a light unto my path*" (King James Version).

King Henry VI continued, "And go in peace, Humphrey, Duke of Gloucester, no less beloved than when you were Lord Protector to your King."

Queen Margaret said, "I see no reason why a King who is no longer a minor should need to be protected like a child. May God and King Henry VI govern England's realm. Give up your staff, sir, and the King's realm."

"Give up my staff?" the Duke of Gloucester said. "Here, noble King Henry VI, is my staff. I resign the staff as willingly as ever your father, King Henry V, made it mine; and even as willingly at your feet I leave it as others would ambitiously receive it.

"Farewell, good King. When I am dead and gone, may honorable peace attend your throne!"

The Duke of Gloucester exited.

Queen Margaret said, "Why, now Henry VI is King, and Margaret is Queen. Humphrey, Duke of Gloucester, is scarcely himself because he bears so severe a maim. Two things at once have been pulled away from him: His lady has been banished, and a limb — his staff of office as Lord Protector — has been lopped off.

"This staff of honor snatched away from him, there let it stand, where it best is suitable to be, in King Henry VI's hand."

The Duke of Suffolk said, "Thus droops this lofty pine and thus hang his branches. Thus Eleanor's pride dies in her youngest — most recent — days."

"Lords, let him go and stop talking about him," the Duke of York said. "If it pleases your majesty, this is the day appointed for the trial by combat, and the appellant and defendant — the armorer and his apprentice — are ready to enter the area of combat, if your highness would like to see the fight."

"Yes, my good lord," Queen Margaret answered for King Henry VI, "because for this purpose I left the court. I want to see this quarrel tried by combat."

King Henry VI said, "In God's name, see that the area of combat and all things are ready. Here let them end it; and may God defend the person who is in the right!"

The Duke of York said, "I never saw a fellow worse prepared, or more afraid to fight, than is the appellant, the apprentice of this armorer, my lords."

From one direction came Horner the armorer and his neighbors, who were drinking to and with him so much that he was drunk. A drummer accompanied them, and Horner carried a staff with a sandbag fastened to one end. This weapon was lethal.

From another direction came Peter the apprentice, also with a drummer and a staff with a sandbag fastened to one end. Some apprentices accompanied and drank to him, but Peter abstained from drinking.

Horner's first neighbor said, "Here, neighbor Horner, I drink to you a cup of the wine called sack, and fear not, neighbor Horner, you shall do well enough in the trial by combat."

Horner's second neighbor said, "And here, neighbor Horner, here's a cup of the wine called charneco."

Horner's third neighbor said, "And here's a pot of good double-strong beer, neighbor Horner. Drink, and don't be afraid of your apprentice."

Horner said, "Let the bowl of alcohol come to me, in faith, and I'll drink to the health of you all, and here's a fig for Peter!"

He made an obscene gesture in Peter's direction.

The first apprentice said, "Here, Peter, I drink to you, and don't be afraid."

The second apprentice said, "Be merry, Peter, and don't be afraid of your master. Fight for the credit and reputation of the apprentices."

"I thank you all," Peter said. "Drink, and pray for me, I ask you, because I think that I have taken my last drink in this world.

"Here, Robin, if I die, I give you my apron.

"And, Will, you shall have my hammer.

"And here, Tom, take all the money that I have.

"Oh, may the Lord bless me, so I pray to God! I am never able to deal with my master in combat because he has learned so much fencing already."

The Earl of Salisbury said, "Come, stop your drinking, and fall to blows.

"Sirrah, what's your name?"

"Peter, indeed."

"Peter! What the rest of your name?"

"Thump," Peter Thump said.

"Thump!" the Earl of Salisbury said. "Then see you thump your master well."

Horner said, "Masters, I have come here, as it were, upon my apprentice's instigation, to prove that he is a knave and that I myself am an honest man. Concerning the Duke of York, I will stake my death that I never meant him any ill, nor the King, nor the Queen.

"Therefore, Peter, I will come at you with a blow directed straight at you!"

"Let's get started," the Duke of York said. "This knave's tongue begins to slur and double the time it takes him to say anything.

"Sound, trumpeters, the call to battle to the combatants!"

Horner and Peter fought, and Peter struck Horner a mortal blow.

Horner shouted, "Stop, Peter, stop! I confess, I confess treason. I am a traitor."

He died.

This culture believed in the importance of confessing sins before dying. Doing so could keep one's soul out of Hell.

"Take away the apprentice's weapon," the Duke of York said.

He then said to Peter, "Fellow, thank God, and the good wine that stood in your master's way and kept him from doing what he was capable of doing while sober."

Overjoyed, Peter said, "Oh, God, have I overcome my enemy in the presence of this royal assembly? Oh, Peter, you have prevailed in combat and proven that you are in the right!"

King Henry VI ordered, "Go, take that traitor away from here and out of our sight. From the fact of his death we perceive his guilt, and God in justice has revealed to us the truth and innocence of this poor fellow named Peter, whom Horner, the traitor, had wanted to have murdered wrongfully in the trial by combat.

"Come, fellow, follow us and receive your reward."

— 2.4 —

The Duke of Gloucester and his servingmen stood on a street. They were wearing hooded cloaks that were customarily worn by mourners.

The Duke of Gloucester said, "Thus sometimes the brightest day has a cloud; and after summer always and forevermore succeeds barren winter with its wrathful and nipping cold. So worries and joys abound, as seasons pass quickly.

"Sirs, what's the time?"

The servants replied, "Ten o'clock, my lord."

"Ten is the hour that was appointed to me to watch the coming of my punished Duchess. She is scarcely able to endure the flinty streets as she treads on them with her unshod and tender-feeling feet.

"Sweet Nell, your noble mind can ill endure the mean-spirited people gazing on your face with their malicious looks, laughing at your shame. These mean-spirited people formerly followed your proud chariot-wheels when you rode in triumph through the streets.

"But, wait! I think she is coming, and I'll prepare my tear-stained eyes to see her miseries."

The Duchess of Gloucester arrived. She was barefoot and wearing a white sheet. In her hand she carried a lit candle. On her back were pinned papers listing the crimes for which she was being punished. With her were Sir John Stanley, the Sheriff, and some officers. Sir John Stanley would take her to the Isle of Man after her public humiliation.

A servant said to the Duke of Gloucester, "If it would please your grace, we'll take her by force from the Sheriff."

"No, don't do that, for your lives; let her pass by," the Duke of Gloucester said.

Seeing him, the Duchess of Gloucester said, "Did you come, my lord, to see my public shame? Now you do penance, too. Look at how they gaze at you! See how the giddy multitude point, and nod their heads, and throw their eyes on you! Ah, Gloucester, hide yourself from their hateful looks, and, pent up in your private chamber, rue my shame, and ban your enemies — both my and your enemies!"

"Be patient and calm, gentle Nell," the Duke of Gloucester said. "Forget this grief."

"Ah, Gloucester, teach me to forget myself!" the Duchess of Gloucester replied. "For while I think I am your married wife and you are a Prince, the Lord Protector of this land, I think I should not thus be led along, wrapped in a white sheet in shame, with papers on my back, and followed by a rabble who rejoice to see my tears and hear my deep-fetched groans. The ruthless flint of the street cuts my tender feet, and when I flinch from the pain, the malicious people laugh and tell me to be careful how I walk.

"Ah, Humphrey, can I bear this shameful yoke? Do you think that I'll ever look upon the world or count people happy who enjoy the Sun?

"No. Dark shall be my light and night shall be my day; to think upon my nobility shall be my Hell.

"Sometimes I'll say that I am Duke Humphrey's wife and he is a Prince and the ruler of the land, yet he so ruled and he was such a Prince that he stood by while I, his forlorn Duchess, was made a spectacle and a pointing-stock to every idle rascal follower.

"But be mild and do not blush at my shame, and do not stir at anything until the axe of death hangs over you, as, surely, it shortly will.

"The Duke of Suffolk, who can do all in all with her, Margaret, who hates you and hates us all, and the Duke of York and impious Cardinal Beaufort, that false priest, have all limed bushes to betray your wings, and, flee however you can, they'll entangle you — they have set a trap for you."

Sarcastically, she added, "But don't be afraid until your foot is snared, and do not seek to prevent your foes from acting."

"Ah, Nell, stop!" the Duke of Gloucester said. "Your aim is all awry; you are mistaken. I must offend before I can be accused and condemned. And if I had twenty times as many foes, and each of them had twenty times their power, all these could not procure for me any harm as long as I am loyal, true, and crimeless.

"Do you want me to rescue you from this reproach? Why, if I did, your scandal would still not be wiped away, but I would be in danger for the breach of law.

"The thing that can best help you is patience and calmness, gentle Nell. Please, make your heart be patient. These few days' wonder will be quickly worn away and exhausted."

A herald arrived and said to the Duke of Gloucester, "I summon your grace to his majesty's Parliament, which will be held at Bury St. Edmunds the first of this next month."

The Duke of Gloucester said, "And I was not asked in advance if I consented to attend the Parliament! I am ordered to be there! This is underhanded plotting! Well, I will be there."

The herald exited.

The Duke of Gloucester said, "My Nell, I take my leave of you, and, master Sheriff, don't let her penance exceed what the King ordered."

The Sheriff replied, "If it pleases your grace, here my orders end, and Sir John Stanley is appointed now to take her with him to the Isle of Man."

The Duke of Gloucester asked, "Must you, Sir John, be the escort of my lady here?"

"So are my orders, may it please your grace," Sir John Stanley replied.

"Don't treat her worse because I ask you to treat her well," the Duke of Gloucester said. "The world may laugh again and look favorably upon me, and I may live to treat you kindly if you treat her kindly, and so, Sir John, farewell!"

The Duchess of Gloucester said, "Are you going, my lord, and without telling me farewell!"

"Witness my tears," the Duke of Gloucester said. "I cannot stay to speak to you."

The Duke of Gloucester and his servingmen exited.

The Duchess of Gloucester said, "Have you gone, too? May all comfort go with you! For none abides with me. My joy is death — death, at whose name I often have been afraid because I wished to enjoy this world for eternity.

"Stanley, please, go, and take me away from here. I don't care where we go, for I beg no favor. Just convey me where you have been commanded to escort me."

"Why, madam, that is to the Isle of Man," Sir John Stanley said. "There you will be treated according to your state."

"That's bad enough, for I am only a source of shame, a person who deserves reproach. Shall I then be treated reproachfully?"

Sir John Stanley replied, "You will be treated like a Duchess, and like Duke Humphrey's lady and wife. According to that state, you shall be treated."

The Duchess of Gloucester said, "Sheriff, farewell, and may you fare better than I fare, although you have been the guide of my walk of shame."

"It was my duty," the Sheriff said, "and, madam, pardon me."

She said, "Yes, yes, farewell, your duty has been discharged.

"Come, Stanley, shall we go?"

Sir John Stanley replied, "Madam, your penance is done, so you will throw off this sheet; we will go to where you can dress yourself for our journey."

"My shame will not be shifted with my sheet," the Duchess of Gloucester said. "I can change what I wear, but my shame will hang upon my richest robes and show itself, no matter how I dress.

"Go, lead the way. I long to see my prison."

CHAPTER 3

— 3.1 —

In the Abbey at Bury St. Edmund's, several people walked into the Parliament: King Henry VI, Queen Margaret, Cardinal Beaufort, the Duke of Suffolk, the Duke of York, the Duke of Buckingham, the Earl of Salisbury, and the Earl of Warwick. Attendants and guards were also present.

King Henry VI said, "I wonder why my Lord of Gloucester has not come. It is not his custom to be the last man to arrive, whatever reason keeps him from us now."

"Can you not see?" Queen Margaret said. "Or will you not observe the aloofness of his altered countenance? With what majesty he bears himself? How insolent and disdainful he has recently become? How proud, how peremptory and dictatorial, and unlike himself?

"We know the time when he was mild and affable, and if we did but cast a far-off look at him, immediately he was upon his knee, so that all the court admired him for his submission.

"But meet him now, and if it is in the morning, when everyone will give each other the time of day and exchange greetings, he knits his brow and shows an angry eye, and passes by with stiff unbowed knee, disdaining to do the respect that belongs to us.

"Small curs are not regarded when they grin — snarl and show their teeth — but great men tremble when the lion roars, and Humphrey, Duke of Gloucester, is no little man in England.

"First note that he is near you in descent, and should you fall, he as the next of kin will mount the throne. To me it seems not to be politically wise, considering what a rancorous mind he bears toward us and his advantage that would follow your decease, that he should come about your royal person or be admitted to your highness' council.

"By using flattery the Duke of Gloucester won the hearts of the common people, and when he pleases to stir up insurrection, it is to be feared they all will follow him.

"Now it is the spring, and weeds are shallowly rooted. Tolerate them now, and they'll overgrow the garden and choke the herbs for want of husbandry and good management.

"The reverent care I bear unto my lord — you, Henry VI — made me see these dangers in the Duke of Gloucester.

"If this is foolish, call it a woman's fear. If better reasoning and evidence can supplant this fear, I will concur and say I wronged the Duke of Gloucester.

"My Lords of Suffolk, Buckingham, and York, disprove my allegation, if you can, or else conclude that my words are to the point."

The Duke of Suffolk said, "Well has your highness seen into this Duke of Gloucester, and if I had been the first to speak my mind, I think I would have told your grace's tale — I would have said what you said.

"The Duchess of Gloucester, I swear upon my life, began her Devilish practices because of his subornation. Or, if he were not privy to those sins and crimes, yet through his holding in esteem his high descent, as being next of kin to the King he is next in succession to the throne if the King dies without children, and through his high boasts about his nobility, he instigated the bedlam — insane — brain-sick Duchess by wicked means to plan our sovereign's fall.

"Smooth runs the water where the brook is deep, and in his simple show — appearance of being an honest man — he harbors treason. The fox does not bark when it wants to steal the lamb.

"No, no, my sovereign. The Duke of Gloucester is a man unsounded and with still unrevealed depths, and he is full of deep deceit."

Cardinal Beaufort said, "Didn't he, contrary to the form of law, order strange, cruel, and unusual deaths as punishment for small offences?"

The Duke of York said, "And didn't he, in his Lord Protectorship, levy great sums of money through the realm of England for soldiers' pay in France, and never sent it? Because of this, the towns each day revolted."

The Duke of Buckingham said, "Tut, these are petty faults in comparison to faults unknown. Time will bring to light these unknown faults that lie in smooth Duke Humphrey."

Using the royal plural, King Henry VI said, "My lords, I will say at once that the concern you have about us that makes you want to mow down thorns that would annoy our foot is worthy of praise, but I shall speak my conscience and say that our kinsman the Duke of Gloucester is as innocent of intending treason to our royal person as is the sucking lamb or harmless dove.

"The Duke of Gloucester is virtuous, mild, and too well disposed to dream about evil or to work toward my downfall."

Queen Margaret said, "Ah, what's more dangerous than this foolish confidence and trust!

"Does the Duke of Gloucester seem to be a dove? His feathers are only borrowed, for his disposition is that of the hateful raven.

"Does he seem to be a lamb? His skin is surely lent him, for his inclination is that of the ravenous wolf.

"Who cannot steal a shape that means deceit? The deceitful man can assume a fake appearance.

"Take heed, my lord; be careful. The welfare of us all hangs on the cutting short that fraudulent man."

One way to cut a man short is to behead him; this will shorten him by a head.

The Duke of Somerset entered and said, "I wish all health to my gracious sovereign!"

"Welcome, Lord Somerset," King Henry VI said. "What is the news from France?"

As Regent of France, the Duke of Somerset was responsible for ruling and protecting the King's territories in France.

"That all your interest in those territories is utterly taken away from you; all is lost."

"This is cold news, Lord Somerset," King Henry VI said, "but God's will be done!"

The Duke of York thought, *This is cold news for me, for I had hope of obtaining France as firmly as I hope to obtain fertile England. Thus are my blossoms blasted in the bud and caterpillars eat my leaves away, but I will remedy this business before long, or sell my title for a glorious grave.*

The Duke of Gloucester arrived and said, "All happiness unto my lord the King! Pardon me, my liege, for having stayed away so long."

The Duke of Suffolk said, "No, Duke of Gloucester, know that you have come too soon, unless you were more loyal than you are. I arrest you on a charge of high treason here."

The Duke of Gloucester replied, "Well, Duke of Suffolk, you shall not see me blush or change my countenance as a result of this arrest.

"A heart unspotted by sin or crime is not easily daunted. The purest spring is not so free from mud as I am clear from treason to my sovereign.

"Who can accuse me? Of what am I supposed to be guilty?"

The Duke of York said, "It is thought, my lord, that you took bribes from the King of France, and as Lord Protector, you kept back the soldiers' pay with the result that his highness has lost France."

"Is it only thought so?" the Duke of Gloucester said. "Who are they who think it?

"I never robbed the soldiers of their pay, nor ever had even one penny as a bribe from the King of France.

"So help me God, I have stayed awake all night, yes, night after night, in studying how to do good for England.

"May any doit — small coin — that ever I wrested from the King, or any groat — another small coin — I hoarded to my use, be brought against me on the Day of Judgment!

"No; many pounds of my own personal money, because I would not tax the needy common people, have I disbursed to the garrisons, and I have never asked for restitution."

Cardinal Beaufort said, "It serves you well, my lord, to say so much."

"I say no more than what is the truth, so help me God!" the Duke of Gloucester said.

The Duke of York said, "In your Lord Protectorship, you devised strange tortures never heard of for offenders, with the result that England was defamed and dishonored by your tyranny."

The Duke of Gloucester replied, "Why, it is well known that, while I was Lord Protector, pity was the only fault that was in me, for I would melt at an offender's tears, and humble, submissive words were the ransom for the offenders' crime.

"Unless it were a bloody murderer, or a foul, felonious thief who fleeced poor travelers, I never gave them their deserved punishment. Murder indeed, that bloody sin, I tortured more than other felonies or crimes."

The Duke of Suffolk said, "My lord, these faults are easily and quickly answered, but mightier crimes are laid to your charge, whereof you cannot easily purge yourself. I arrest you in his highness' name, and here I commit you to my lord Cardinal Beaufort to keep under guard until your future time of trial."

King Henry VI said, "My lord of Gloucester, it is my special hope that you will clear yourself from all suspicion. My conscience tells me you are innocent."

"Ah, gracious lord, these days are dangerous," the Duke of Gloucester said. "Virtue is choked with foul ambition and charity is chased away from here by rancor's hand. Foul subornation is in the ascendant and justice has been exiled from your highness' land.

"I know that their plot is to have my life, and if my death might make this island happy, and prove to be the end of their tyranny, I would expend my life with all willingness. But my death is made the prologue to their play, for the deaths of thousands more, who yet suspect no peril, will not conclude their plotted tragedy.

"Cardinal Beaufort's red sparkling eyes blab and betray his heart's malice, and the Duke of Suffolk's cloudy appearance blabs and betrays his stormy hate. Sharp Buckingham unburdens with his tongue the envious load that lies upon his heart, and dogged, spiteful York, who reaches at the moon and at other things it is impossible to get, whose overweening arm I have plucked back, by false accusation aims at my life. And you, my sovereign lady, my Queen, along with the rest, without justification have laid disgraces on my head, and with your best efforts have stirred up my most cherished liege — Henry VI — to be my enemy.

"Yes, all of you have laid your heads together — I myself had notice of your secret meetings — all to take away my guiltless life.

"I shall not lack false witnesses to condemn me, nor shall I lack an abundance of 'treasons' attributed to me to augment my guilt.

"The ancient proverb will be well fulfilled: 'A staff is quickly found to beat a dog.'"

Cardinal Beaufort said to King Henry VI, "My liege, his railing is intolerable. If those who care to keep your royal person from treason's secret knife and traitors' rage be thus upbraided, criticized, and berated, and the offender be granted scope of speech, it will make them cool in zeal toward your grace."

The Duke of Suffolk said, "Has he not taunted our sovereign lady the Queen here with ignominious words, though clerkly couched — learnedly expressed — as if she had suborned some to swear false allegations to overthrow his greatness?"

Queen Margaret said, "But I can give the loser permission to chide and scold."

The Duke of Gloucester said, "That is far truer spoken than meant. I lose, indeed. Damn the winners, for they have played me false! They have betrayed me! And well such losers may have permission to speak."

The Duke of Buckingham said, "He'll twist the meaning of whatever we say and hold us here all day.

"Lord Cardinal Beaufort, he is your prisoner."

Cardinal Beaufort ordered, "Sirs, take away the Duke of Gloucester, and guard him securely."

The Duke of Gloucester said, "Ah! Thus King Henry VI throws away his crutch before his legs are robust enough to bear his body. Thus is the shepherd beaten from your side, and wolves are snarling over who shall gnaw you first. Ah, I wish that my fear were false! Ah, I wish that it were! For, good King Henry, I fear that you will be destroyed."

Guards took away the Duke of Gloucester.

King Henry VI said, "My lords, whatever your wisdoms think to be best, do or not do, just as if we ourself were here."

Queen Margaret asked, "Will your highness leave the Parliament?"

"Yes, Margaret," King Henry VI said. "My heart is drowned with grief, whose flood begins to flow within my eyes. My body is engirdled by misery, for what's more miserable than discontent?

"Ah, uncle Humphrey! In your face I see the embodiment of honor, truth, and loyalty. Good Humphrey, Duke of Gloucester, the hour is yet to come that ever I experienced you being traitorous or I feared your loyalty. What louring, ominous star now envies your high rank and standing, with the result that these great lords and Margaret our Queen seek the destruction of your harmless life? You never did them wrong, nor did you ever do any man wrong.

"Just like the butcher takes away the calf and binds the wretch, and beats it when it strays, bearing it to the bloody slaughterhouse, even so remorselessly have they borne the Duke of Gloucester away from here, and as the mother of the calf runs lowing up and down, looking in the direction her harmless young one went, and can do nothing but bewail her darling's loss, even so I myself bewail good Gloucester's case with sad, unhelpful tears, and with dimmed eyes look after him and cannot do him any good, so mighty are his vowed enemies.

"His fortunes I will weep, and in between each groan I will say, 'Who's a traitor? Gloucester is not a traitor.'"

Everyone exited except Queen Margaret, Cardinal Beaufort, the Duke of Suffolk, and the Duke of York. The Duke of Somerset stayed, but he watched the others and did not take place in their plotting.

Queen Margaret said, "Free, honorable, worthy lords, cold snow melts with the Sun's hot beams. My lord — Henry VI — is cold in great affairs. He is too full of foolish pity, and the Duke of Gloucester's performance beguiles him as the mournful crocodile with its crocodile tears of sorrow snares soft-hearted travelers — it cries to entice travelers to come near it, and then it snatches at them — or as the snake coiled in a flowering bank, with shining, multicolored skin, bites a child who thinks the snake is excellent because of its beauty.

"Believe me, lords, if no one were wiser than I — and yet herein I judge my own intelligence to be good — this Duke of Gloucester would be quickly rid — removed from — the world, in order to rid — free — us of the fear we have of him."

Cardinal Beaufort said, "That the Duke of Gloucester should die is a sensible policy and good statesmanship, but yet we need a pretext for his death. It is a good idea for him to be condemned by the course of law."

The Duke of Suffolk said, "But, in my mind, that would not be a good idea; it won't work. The King will labor always to save the Duke of Gloucester's life. The common people perhaps will rise to save the Duke of Gloucester's life. As of yet we have only trivial evidence, other than mistrust of him, that shows him to deserve a death sentence."

The Duke of York said, "Judging by what you say, you would not have him die."

"Ah, York, no man alive is as eager as I am to see him dead!" the Duke of Suffolk said.

The Duke of York said, "It is I, the Duke of York, who has more reason to want the Duke of Gloucester to die.

"But, my lord Cardinal Beaufort, and you, my Lord of Suffolk, say what you think, and speak it from your souls, isn't it the same thing to set a hungry eagle to guard the chicken from a hungry kite — a bird of prey — and to make Humphrey, Duke of Gloucester, the King's Protector?"

Queen Margaret said, "Either way, the poor chicken would be sure to die."

"Madam, it is true," the Duke of Suffolk said, "and isn't it madness, then, to make the fox the guardian of the sheepfold? Should a person accused of being a crafty murderer have his guilt only frivolously looked at because his purpose is not executed and he has not yet committed the murder? No. Let him die. Why? Because he is a fox. And therefore his nature proves him to be an enemy to the flock even before his jaws are stained with crimson blood. Humphrey, Duke of Gloucester, as proven by this reasoning, is like a fox to my liege: King Henry VI.

"And so we ought not to insist on niceties when it comes to slaying him. The main thing is that he die, whether it be by traps, by snares, by treacherousness, whether sleeping or awake, none of that matters as long as he dies, for good deceit checkmates first the man who first intends deceit."

"Thrice-noble Suffolk, you have resolutely spoken your mind," Queen Margaret said.

The Duke of Suffolk replied, "What I have said is not resolute, except in so much that is done, for things are often spoken about and seldom meant.

"But because my heart accords with my tongue, seeing the deed is meritorious and deserves to be rewarded by God because it will preserve my sovereign the King from his foe, say but the word, and I will be his priest. I will metaphorically give him his last rites — by literally making his last rites necessary."

Cardinal Beaufort said, "But I want him dead, my Lord of Suffolk, before you can take due orders for and become a priest. Say that you consent and judge the deed to be good, and I'll provide an executioner to kill the Duke of Gloucester because I care so much for the safety of my liege the King."

The Duke of Suffolk said, "Here is my hand. The deed is worthy and worth doing."

They shook hands.

Queen Margaret said, "And I also say the deed is worthy and worth doing."

The Duke of York said, "And so do I, and now that we three have agreed with Cardinal Beaufort to have the Duke of Gloucester murdered, it does not much matter who disputes the validity of what we have decided.

A messenger entered the room and said, "Great lords, from Ireland I have come at full speed to report that rebels there are up in arms and have put the Englishmen to the sword. Send reinforcements, lords, and stop the rage quickly before the wound grows incurable because since the rebellion is fresh and green, there is great hope that help can stop it."

Cardinal Beaufort said, "This is a rebellion that needs a quick and expeditious stop!

"What advice do all of you give in this important affair?"

The Duke of York said, "I advise that the Duke of Somerset be sent as Regent there in Ireland. It is fitting that this lucky ruler be employed there. Just look at the fortune he has had in France."

The Duke of York was being sarcastic. While the Duke of Somerset had been Regent in France, all the French regions controlled by England had been lost to the French.

The Duke of Somerset said, "If the Duke of York, with all his scheming and cunning political policy had been the Regent there instead of me, he never would have stayed in France so long."

"No, not to lose it all, as you have done," the Duke of York replied. "I would have lost my life speedily rather than bring a burden of dishonor home by staying there a long time and losing all the English-controlled French territories.

"Show me one scar engraved on your skin. Men whose flesh is preserved so whole seldom win."

Queen Margaret said, "Don't engage in this wrangling. This spark will prove to become a raging fire, if wind and fuel are brought to feed it with.

"Say no more, good York; sweet Somerset, be still and quiet. Your fortune, York, if you had been Regent there, might perhaps have proven to be far worse than his."

"What, worse than nothing?" the Duke of York said. "In that case, then, may a shame take all!"

The Duke of Somerset said, "And among that number of people shamed, count yourself — you who wish shame on others!"

Cardinal Beaufort said, "My Lord of York, try what your fortune is. The uncivilized kerns of Ireland — lightly armed Irish foot soldiers — are in arms and moisten clay with blood of Englishmen. Will you lead a band of men, collected and chosen carefully, some from each county, and try your fortune against the Irishmen?"

"I will, my lord, if it pleases his majesty," the Duke of York said.

The Duke of Suffolk said, "Why, our authority is his consent: Whatever we decide to do he will confirm. So then, noble York, take this task in hand. Take an English army to Ireland."

"I am content," the Duke of York said. "I agree. Provide soldiers for me, lords, while I make arrangements for my own affairs."

"This charge, Lord York, I will see performed," the Duke of Suffolk said. "I will see that you get soldiers. But now we return to the false and traitorous Humphrey, Duke of Gloucester."

Cardinal Beaufort said, "We need talk no more about him, for I will deal with him in such a way that henceforth he shall trouble us no more.

"And so let us break off our meeting; the day is almost spent.

"Lord Suffolk, you and I must talk of that event. I will get the murderers and you will tell them what to do and how to do it."

The Duke of York said, "My Lord of Suffolk, within fourteen days I will expect my soldiers to be at Bristol because from there I'll ship them all to Ireland."

"I'll see it truly done, my Lord of York," the Duke of Suffolk said.

Everyone exited except the Duke of York, who began speaking to himself:

"Now, York, or never, steel your fearful, apprehensive thoughts, and change doubtfulness to resolution. Be what you hope to be, or resign to death what you are — it is not worth the enjoying. Let pale-faced fear stay with the lowly born man, and find no harbor in a royal heart.

"Faster than springtime showers comes thought on thought, and every thought thinks about high rank. My brain more busily than the laboring spider weaves wearyingly intricate snares to trap my enemies.

"Well, nobles, well, it is shrewdly done, to send me packing with an army of men. I fear that you are only warming the frozen snake that, once warmed against your chests, will sting your hearts.

"It was men I lacked and you will give them to me. I take this army kindly; and yet be well assured that you are putting sharp weapons in a madman's hands.

"While I in Ireland nourish a mighty band of soldiers, I will stir up in England some black storm that shall blow ten thousand souls to Heaven or Hell, and this fell tempest shall not cease to rage until the golden circle is placed on my head — a crown like the glorious Sun's transparent beams will calm the fury of this mad-bred squall. This squall will be produced by a madman — me.

"And, for the agent of my intention, I have persuaded a headstrong Kentish man, John Cade of Ashford, whose nickname is Jack, to make a rebellion, as he very well is capable of doing, while pretending to be John Mortimer.

"In Ireland I have seen this stubborn, ruthless, fierce Cade oppose himself against a troop of Irish kerns, and he fought so long that his thighs with darts — arrows and light spears — were almost like a sharp-quilled porcupine.

"And, after he was finally rescued, I have seen him caper upright like a wild Morris dancer, shaking the bloody darts as the Morris dancer shakes his bells.

"Very often, disguised as a shaggy-haired crafty Irish kern, he has conversed with the enemy, and undiscovered come back to me again and given me notice of their villainies.

"This Devil — John Cade — here shall be my substitute because John Cade resembles in face, in gait, and in speech John Mortimer, who now is dead.

"By this I shall perceive the commoners' minds, how they think about the House and claim of York to the crown. If they follow John Cade, they will follow me.

"Let's say that John Cade is captured and tortured on the rack. I know that no pain they can inflict upon him will make him say I persuaded him to take up those weapons.

"Let's say that he thrives, as it is very likely he will, why, then from Ireland I will come with my strong army and reap the harvest that the rascal John Cade has sowed.

"With Humphrey, Duke of Gloucester, dead, as he shall be, and Henry VI put aside, then the next King of England will be me."

Some murderers entered a room of state at Bury St. Edmund's. They had just murdered the Duke of Gloucester by strangling him.

The first murderer said, "Run to my Lord of Suffolk; let him know that we have dispatched the Duke of Gloucester, as he commanded."

"Oh, that it were not yet done so that we could decide not to do it!" the second murderer said. "What have we done! Did you ever hear a man so penitent?"

The Duke of Suffolk entered the room.

The murderer said, "Here comes my Lord of Suffolk."

"Now, sirs, have you dispatched this thing?" the Duke of Suffolk asked. "Have you murdered him?"

"Yes, my good lord, he's dead," the first murderer said.

"Why, that's well done," the Duke of Suffolk said. "Go to my house; I will reward you for this venturous, dangerous deed. The King and all the peers are here at hand. Have you remade the bed? Is everything done well, in accordance with the directions I gave you?"

"Yes, it is, my good lord," the first murderer said.

"Leave! Be gone!" the Duke of Suffolk ordered.

The murderers exited.

Trumpets sounded, and several people entered the room: King Henry VI, Queen Margaret, Cardinal Beaufort, the Duke of Somerset, and some attendants.

King Henry VI said, "Go, call our uncle the Duke of Gloucester to come into our presence immediately. Say that we intend to try his grace today to determine whether he is guilty, as charged publicly."

The Duke of Suffolk said, "I'll call him to you immediately, my noble lord."

He exited.

King Henry VI said, "Lords, take your places, and I ask you all to proceed no stricter against our uncle the Duke of Gloucester than from true evidence of good value he is proven to be guilty of treachery. Let true evidence of good value show whether he is guilty or innocent."

Queen Margaret said, "May God forbid that any malice should prevail that would condemn an innocent nobleman! I pray to God that the Duke of Gloucester may acquit himself of suspicion!"

"I thank you, Meg," King Henry VI said. "These words much content me. They make me very happy."

The Duke of Suffolk reentered the room.

Seeing him, King Henry VI said, "What's going on! Why do you look pale? Why are you trembling? Where is our uncle the Duke of Gloucester? What's the matter, Suffolk?"

"He is dead in his bed, my lord," the Duke of Suffolk said. "The Duke of Gloucester is dead."

"By the Virgin Mary, God forbid!" Queen Margaret said.

Cardinal Beaufort said, "This is God's secret judgment. I dreamt last night that the Duke of Gloucester was mute and could not speak a word."

King Henry VI fainted.

"How is my lord?" Queen Margaret said. "Help, lords! The King is dead."

"Raise his body," the Duke of Somerset said. "Wring his nose."

This was thought to help someone regain consciousness.

"Run, go, help, help!" Queen Margaret said. "Henry, open your eyes!"

"He is regaining consciousness," the Duke of Suffolk said. "Madam, be calm."

"Oh, Heavenly God!" King Henry VI said.

"How is my gracious lord?" Queen Margaret asked.

"Take comfort, my sovereign!" the Duke of Suffolk said. "Gracious Henry, take comfort!"

"Is my Lord of Suffolk comforting me?" King Henry VI said sarcastically to him. "He came just now to sing a raven's ominous note of death, whose dismal tune took away from me my vital powers, and does he think that the chirping of a wren, crying 'take comfort' from a hollow, false, insincere breast, can chase away the first-heard sound — that of the raven?

"Don't hide your poison with such sugared words. Lay not your hands on me; stop and forbear, I say. The touch of your hands frightens me as much as a serpent's bite.

"You baleful messenger, get out of my sight! Upon your eyeballs murderous tyranny sits in grim majesty and frightens the world.

"Don't look upon me — your eyes wound me.

"Yet do not go away. Come, basilisk, and kill the innocent gazer with your sight, for in the shadow of death I shall find joy. In life I find only double death, now that the Duke of Gloucester is dead."

A basilisk is a mythological serpent that could kill people simply by looking at them.

Queen Margaret said, "Why do you berate my Lord of Suffolk thus? Although the Duke of Gloucester was his enemy, yet Suffolk like a Christian laments his death. And as for myself, foe as the Duke of Gloucester was to me, if liquid tears or heart-offending groans or blood-consuming sighs could recall his life, I would be blind with weeping, sick with groans, and look as pale as a primrose with blood-drinking sighs, and all to have the noble Duke of Gloucester alive."

She was referring to the belief that each sigh or groan would take a drop of blood away from the heart.

Queen Margaret continued, "What do I know about how the world may judge of me? It is known that the Duke of Gloucester and I were only hollow friends — we were enemies. It may be judged I killed the Duke, and so shall my name be wounded by the tongue of slander, and Princes' courts be filled with the reproach of me. This is what I get by his death — unhappy me! To be a Queen, and crowned with infamy!"

King Henry VI said, "Ah, woe is me for Gloucester, wretched man! I am grieved because of his death."

Queen Margaret said, "Be woe for me — be sorry for me — because I am more wretched than he is. Do you turn away from me and hide your face? I am no loathsome leper; look at me.

"What! Are you, like the adder, grown deaf? Be poisonous like the adder and kill your forlorn Queen."

Ebenezer Cobham Brewer's *Dictionary of Phrase and Fable* states, "According to tradition, the asp stops its ears when the charmer utters his incantation, by applying one ear to the ground and twisting its tail into the other."

Psalm 58:3-5 (King James Version) states this:

3 *The wicked are estranged from the womb: they go astray as soon as they be born, speaking lies.*

4 Their poison is like the poison of a serpent: they are like the deaf adder that stoppeth her ear;

5 Which will not hearken to the voice of charmers, charming never so wisely.

Queen Margaret continued, "Is all your comfort shut in the Duke of Gloucester's tomb? Why, then, Dame Margaret was never your joy. Erect his statue and worship it, and make my image just a cheap alehouse sign.

"Was I for this almost wrecked upon the sea and twice by adverse winds from England's bank driven back again to my native land? What foretold this, but a well-meaning and accurately prophesizing forewarning wind that seemed to say 'Don't seek a scorpion's nest, and don't set foot on this unkind shore'?

"What did I then, but cursed the gentle gusts and Aeolus, the god of winds, who loosed them forth from their strong bronze caves. And I bade the winds to blow towards England's blessed shore or turn our stern upon a dreadful rock and wreck the ship and drown me.

"Yet Aeolus would not be a murderer but left that hateful office to you. The pretty vaulting — rising and falling — sea refused to drown me, knowing that you would have me drowned on shore, with tears as salty as sea water, through your unkindness. The rocks that split ships in pieces cowered in the sinking sands and would not dash me with their jagged sides so that your flinty heart, harder than they, might in your palace destroy me, Margaret.

"As long as I could see your chalky cliffs at Dover, when from your shore the tempest beat us back, I stood upon the deck in the storm, and when the dusky sky began to rob my eagerly peering sight of the view of your land, I took a costly jeweled ornament from my neck — a heart it was, surrounded by diamonds — and threw it towards your land. The sea received it, and so I wished your body might receive my heart. And even with this I lost sight of fair England and bade my eyes to depart with my heart and called my eyes blind and dusky spectacles because they lost sight of Albion's — England's — wished-for coast.

"How often have I tempted Suffolk's tongue, the agent of your foul inconstancy, the one who convinced me to marry you, to sit and bewitch me, as Ascanius did when he to Dido, maddened by love, would unfold his father's acts commenced in burning Troy!"

In Virgil's *Aeneid*, Aeneas' son, Ascanius (actually Venus' disguised son Cupid took his place) sat on the lap of Dido, Queen of Carthage, and told her about the exploits of Aeneas, who had survived the fall of Troy and rescued his father and son from the burning city.

Queen Margaret continued, "Am I not bewitched like her? Are you not false like him?"

Aeneas and Dido had a love affair in Carthage, but Aeneas left her in order to go to Italy and achieve his destiny of being an important ancestor of the Roman people.

Queen Margaret continued, "Woe is me. I can say or do no more! Die, Margaret, because Henry weeps that you live so long."

Noises were heard, and the Earl of Warwick and the Earl of Salisbury entered the room. Many commoners stood outside the room.

The Earl of Warwick said to King Henry VI, "It is reported, mighty sovereign, that the good Humphrey, Duke of Gloucester, has been traitorously murdered by the means of the Duke of Suffolk and Cardinal Beaufort. The commoners, like an angry hive of bees that want their leader, scatter up and down and care not whom they sting in seeking revenge for his death. I myself have calmed their spleenful mutiny, until they hear the manner of his death."

"That he is dead, good Warwick, is too true," King Henry VI said. "But how he died God knows, not I, Henry. Enter his chamber, view his breathless corpse, and then tell us your opinion of his sudden death."

"That I shall do, my liege," the Earl of Warwick said. "Stay, Salisbury, with the unrefined multitude until I return."

The Earl of Warwick exited and joined the commoners.

King Henry VI said, "Oh, You Who judges all things, keep back my thoughts, my thoughts that labor to persuade my soul that some violent hands were laid on Humphrey's life! If my suspicion is false, forgive me, God, because judgment belongs only to You.

"Gladly would I go to warm the Duke of Gloucester's pale lips with twenty thousand kisses, and to rain upon his face an ocean of salt tears, to tell my love and friendship for him to his silent deaf body, and with my fingers feel his unfeeling hand. But all in vain are these mean funeral obsequies, and to survey his dead and Earthly image, what would it accomplish except to make my sorrow greater?"

The Earl of Warwick and some others came into the room, carrying the bed on which lay the corpse of the Duke of Gloucester.

The Earl of Warwick said to King Henry VI, "Come here, gracious sovereign, and view this body."

"That is to see how deep my grave is made," King Henry VI said, "for with his soul fled all my worldly solace. When I see him, I see my life in death."

The Earl of Warwick said, "As surely as my soul intends to live with that revered King — Jesus, our Lord and Savior — Who took our state upon him to free us from His Father's wrathful curse as recounted in Genesis, I believe that violent hands were laid upon the life of this much-famed Duke of Gloucester."

Genesis 3:17-19 (King James Version) states this:

17 *And unto Adam he said, Because thou hast hearkened unto the voice of thy wife, and hast eaten of the tree, of which I commanded thee, saying, Thou shalt not eat of it: cursed is the ground for thy sake; in sorrow shalt thou eat of it all the days of thy life;*

18 *Thorns also and thistles shall it bring forth to thee; and thou shalt eat the herb of the field;*

19 *In the sweat of thy face shalt thou eat bread, till thou return unto the ground; for out of it wast thou taken: for dust thou art, and unto dust shalt thou return.*

"That is a dreadful oath, sworn with a solemn tongue!" the Duke of Suffolk said. "What evidence does Lord Warwick give for his vow?"

The Earl of Warwick said, "See how the blood is settled in his face. Often I have seen a body that has died a natural death have an ashy appearance, pale and bloodless, because the blood has all descended to the laboring heart. The heart, in the conflict that it wages with death, attracts the blood for aid against the enemy — death. The blood stays in the heart after death and there cools and never returns to blush and beautify the cheek again.

"But look, the Duke of Gloucester's face is black and full of blood. His eyeballs are further out than when he lived; he is staring very ghastly like a strangled man. His hair is standing on end, his nostrils are stretched with struggling; his hands are displayed wide apart, like those of a man who grasped and tugged for life and was by strength subdued.

"Look, you can see his hair is sticking on the sheets. His well-proportioned beard has been made rough and rugged, like the summer's wheat that has been beaten down by a tempest.

"It cannot be otherwise than that he was murdered here. The least of all these signs makes that probable."

The Duke of Suffolk said, "Why, Warwick, who would murder the Duke of Gloucester? I myself and Cardinal Beaufort had him in our protection, and we, I hope, sir, are no murderers."

"But both of you were Duke Humphrey's vowed foes," the Earl of Warwick said.

He then said to Cardinal Beaufort, "And you, certainly, had the good Duke of Gloucester in your custody to guard. It is likely you would not feast him like a friend, and it is easily and clearly seen he found an enemy."

Queen Margaret said, "Then you, it seems, suspect these noblemen to be guilty of Duke Humphrey of Gloucester's untimely death."

The Earl of Warwick said, "A person who finds the heifer dead and freshly bleeding and sees close by a butcher with an axe will definitely suspect it was the butcher who made the slaughter. A person who finds the partridge in the nest of a bird of prey will definitely imagine how the bird died, although the bird of prey soars with an unbloody beak. Even so suspicious is this tragedy."

Queen Margaret asked, "Are you the butcher, Duke of Suffolk? Where's your knife? Is Cardinal Beaufort being called a bird of prey? Where are his talons?"

The Duke of Suffolk said, "I wear no knife to slaughter sleeping men, but here's a vengeful sword, rusted with disuse, that shall be scoured in the rancorous heart of any man who slanders me with murder's crimson badge.

"Say, if you dare, proud Lord of Warwickshire, that I am guilty of the death of Humphrey, Duke of Gloucester."

Cardinal Beaufort's face had become pale at the sight of the corpse of the Duke of Gloucester. Now he was close to fainting, and so the Duke of Somerset and some others assisted him in leaving the room.

The Earl of Warwick replied to the Duke of Suffolk, "What doesn't Warwick dare to do, if false, treacherous Suffolk dares him?"

Queen Margaret said, "He dares not calm his arrogant, insolent, contentious spirit nor cease to be an arrogant critic, although Suffolk dare him twenty thousand times."

"Madam, be quiet," the Earl of Warwick said. "With reverence may I say that every word you speak in Suffolk's behalf is slander to your royal dignity."

"Blunt-witted lord, ignoble in demeanor!" the Duke of Suffolk said. "If ever a lady wronged her lord so much, your mother took into her blameworthy bed some coarse untutored peasant, and noble stock was grafted with a slip from a crabapple tree, whose fruit you are — you were never of the Nevilles' noble family."

The Earl of Warwick said, "Except that the guilt of murder protects you like a buckler, aka a shield, and except that I would rob the deathsman of his fee for executing you for murder, in which act of me killing you I would be acquitting you thereby of ten thousand shames, and except that my sovereign's presence makes me mild, I would, you false murderous coward, make you beg pardon on your knee for your just now expressed speech, and I would make you say it was your mother that you meant and that you yourself were born a bastard. And after all this fearful homage was done, I would give you your hire, aka wages — death — and send your soul to Hell, you pernicious bloodsucker of sleeping men!"

The Duke of Suffolk said, "You shall be awake while I shed your blood, if away from the presence of King Henry VI you dare go with me."

The Earl of Warwick replied, "Let's go away from the King's presence right now, or I will drag you away. Unworthy though you are, I'll fight you and do some service to Duke Humphrey's ghost."

The Duke of Suffolk and the Earl of Warwick exited.

King Henry VI said, "What is a stronger breastplate than an untainted heart! Thrice is that man armed who has a just quarrel, and that man whose conscience is corrupted with injustice is naked, although he is locked up in steel armor."

Noise was heard coming from outside.

Queen Margaret said, "What noise is this?"

The Duke of Suffolk and the Earl of Warwick reentered the room. Both of them had drawn their weapons, which was a serious offense. Drawn weapons were not allowed in the presence of the King.

King Henry VI said, "Why, what are you doing, lords! You have your wrathful weapons drawn here in our presence! Do you dare be so bold? Why, what tumultuous clamor do we have here?"

The Duke of Suffolk said, "The traitorous Warwick with the men of Bury St. Edmunds all set upon me, mighty sovereign."

The Earl of Salisbury and several commoners entered the room.

The Earl of Salisbury said to the commoners, "Sirs, stand outside; the King shall know your mind."

The commoners exited.

He then said to King Henry VI, "Dread lord, the commoners send you word by me that unless Lord Suffolk is immediately executed, or banished from fair England's territories, they will by violence tear him from your palace and torture him with a grievous lingering death. They say that by him the good Humphrey, Duke of Gloucester, died. They say that in him they fear your highness' death; and their pure instinct of love and loyalty, free from a stubborn hostile intent, which might be thought to contradict your liking, makes them thus insistent on his banishment.

"They say out of concern for your most royal person that if your highness would intend to sleep and would order that no man should disturb your rest on pain of your dislike or on pain of death, they still, notwithstanding such a strict edict, would wake you if it were necessary to protect your life.

"For example, if there were a serpent seen, with forked tongue, that slyly glided towards your majesty, and it were necessary to awaken you lest your remaining in that slumber would allow the deadly snake to make your sleep eternal, they therefore would cry out and awaken you, although you forbid them to.

"They say that they will guard you, whether you want them to or not, from such cruel serpents as false Suffolk, with whose envenomed and fatal sting your loving uncle Gloucester, who was worth twenty times the worth of Suffolk, they say, is shamefully bereft of life."

The commoners shouted from outside, "We want an answer from the King, my Lord of Salisbury!"

The Duke of Suffolk said to the Earl of Salisbury, "It is likely that the commoners, rude unpolished peasants, could send such a message to their sovereign. But you, my lord, were glad to be employed, to show how clever an orator you are. But all the honor you, Salisbury, have won is that you are the lord ambassador sent from a gang of tinkers to the King."

In this society, one meaning of the word "tinker" was "beggar."

The commoners shouted from outside the room, "We want an answer from the King, or we will all break in!"

King Henry VI ordered, "Go, Salisbury, and tell them all from me that I thank them for their tender loving care, and even if I had not been incited by them, yet I intended and intend to do what they entreat me to do, for surely my thoughts do hourly prophesy misfortune to my well-being by Suffolk's means.

"And therefore, I swear by His majesty Whose much unworthy deputy I am that Suffolk shall not breathe infection into this air for more than three days longer, on the pain of death."

The Earl of Salisbury left to inform the commoners that the Duke of Suffolk would be exiled from England within three days.

Queen Margaret said, "Oh, Henry, let me plead for gentle Suffolk!"

"Ungentle Queen, to call him gentle Suffolk!" King Henry VI said. "Unkind Queen, to call him kind Suffolk! Plead no more, I say. If you plead for him, you will only increase my wrath.

"Had I but pronounced the sentence, but not sworn to it, I would have kept my word, but when I swear, it is irrevocable."

He said to the Duke of Suffolk, "If, after three days' space, you are found here on any ground that I am ruler of, the world shall not be the ransom for your life."

King Henry VI then said, "Come, Warwick. Come, good Warwick, and go with me. I have great matters to impart to you."

Everyone exited except for Queen Margaret and the Duke of Suffolk.

Queen Margaret said in the direction in which King Henry VI and the Earl of Warwick had departed, "May misfortune and sorrow go along with you! May heart's discontent and sour affliction be playfellows to keep you company! There are two of you; may the Devil make a third! And may threefold vengeance escort your steps!"

The Duke of Suffolk said, "Gentle Queen, stop these imprecations and let your Suffolk take his sorrowful leave."

"Damn, you coward woman and soft-hearted wretch! Haven't you the spirit to curse your enemy?" Queen Margaret said.

"May a plague fall upon them!" the Duke of Suffolk said. "Why should I curse them? If curses would kill, as does the poisonous mandrake's cry when it is pulled from the ground, I would invent as bitter-wounding terms, as angry, as harsh and as horrible to hear, delivered as strongly through my clenched teeth, with as very many signs of deadly hate as the curses that the lean-faced, emaciated hag Envy delivers in her loathsome cave.

"My tongue would stumble as it sought to say my earnest words. My eyes would sparkle like the beaten flint. My hair would be fixed on end, as if I were deranged. Yes, every joint would seem to curse and excommunicate. And even now my burdened heart would break, should I not curse them.

"May poison be their drink! May gall — no, worse than gall — be the most delicious thing that they taste! May their sweetest shade be a grove of cypress trees in a cemetery! May their chief vista be murdering basilisks — either the large cannon known by that name or the snake that kills with a glance! May the softest thing they touch be as painful as a lizard's sting! May their music be as frightful as the serpent's hiss! And may foreboding screech owls make the band of musicians full! May all the foul terrors in dark-situated Hell —"

Queen Margaret interrupted, "Enough, sweet Suffolk. You are tormenting yourself, and these dread curses, like the Sun shining against a mirror, or like a gun filled too full of powder, recoil, and turn their force upon yourself."

The Duke of Suffolk said, "You bade me curse, and will you now tell me to stop? Now, by the ground that I am banished from, I say that I could curse away a winter's night, although I were standing naked on a mountain top, where biting cold would never let grass grow, and I would think it but a minute spent in entertainment."

Queen Margaret said, "Oh, let me entreat you to cease cursing. Give me your hand so that I may dew it with my mournful tears; don't let the rain of Heaven wet this place, to wash away my woeful monuments — the tracks of my tears.

"I wish that this kiss could be printed in your hand so that by the seal you might think upon these lips of mine, through which a thousand sighs are breathed for you!

"So, leave so that I may know my grief, which is only imagined while you are standing by me, as if I were a person who overindulges while thinking about what she wants.

"I will get a repeal of your exile for you, or you can be well assured that I will do what it takes to be banished myself. And I am banished if I am apart from you.

"Go; don't speak to me. Even now be gone."

The Duke of Suffolk started to leave.

Queen Margaret changed her mind: "Oh, don't go yet! Even like this, two friends who are condemned to die will embrace and kiss and take ten thousand leaves, both of them a hundred times loather to part from each other than to die.

"Yet now I say farewell to you; and I say farewell to life as well as to you!"

The Duke of Suffolk said, "Thus is poor Suffolk banished ten times: once by the King, and three times thrice by you. It is not the land I care for, if you were away from here. A wilderness is populous enough, as long as I, Suffolk, would have your Heavenly company. For where you are, there is the world itself, with all the many pleasures in the world, and where you are not, there is desolation.

"I can say and do no more. Live to enjoy your life. I myself find joy in nothing except knowing that you live."

A lord named Vaux arrived.

Queen Margaret asked, "Where is Vaux going so fast? What is your news, please?"

Vaux replied, "To report to his majesty that Cardinal Beaufort is at the point of death, for suddenly a grievous sickness took him that makes him gasp and stare and struggle for breath, blaspheming God and cursing men on Earth.

"Sometimes he talks as if Duke Humphrey of Gloucester's ghost were by his side; sometimes he calls to the King, and whispers to his pillow, as if he were speaking to him, the secrets of his overwrought soul. And I have been sent to tell his majesty that even now he cries aloud for him."

Queen Margaret said, "Go tell this solemn message to the King."

Vaux exited.

Queen Margaret said, "Ay, me! What a world is this! What news is this!

"But why am I grieving about an hour's poor loss? Cardinal Beaufort was an old man, and he would have lived only a short time — call it an hour! — more. Why am I omitting Suffolk's exile, the exile of my soul's treasure? That is the real grief.

"Why don't I mourn only for you, Suffolk, and compete in tears with the southern clouds that bring rain? The southern clouds' tears are for the Earth's crops, while my tears are for my sorrows.

"Now go away from here. The King, you know, is coming. If you are found beside me, you will die."

The Duke of Suffolk replied, "If I depart from you, I cannot live, and what would dying in your sight be like other than taking a pleasant slumber in your lap?"

In this culture, one meaning of "dying" was "orgasming," and one meaning of "lap" was "pudendum."

The Duke of Suffolk continued, "Here I could breathe my soul into the air, as mild and gentle as the cradle-babe dying with its mother's nipple between its lips.

"In contrast, away from your sight, I would be raging mad, and cry out for you to close my eyes — the eyes of a dead man — and to have you with your lips stop my mouth.

"That way, you would either send back my flying soul, or I would breathe my soul into your body and then it would live in sweet Elysium.

"To die beside you would be only to die in jest. To die away from you would be a torture more than death.

"Oh, let me stay, befall what may befall! Let me stay, no matter what happens!"

Queen Margaret said, "Leave! Although parting is a fretful, corrosive cure, it is applied to a deadly wound. If you stay, you die. If you go into exile, you live.

"Go to France, sweet Suffolk. Let me hear from you, for wherever you are in this world's globe, I'll have an Iris — a messenger — who shall find you."

Iris was a messenger for the classical gods.

The Duke of Suffolk said, "I am going."

Queen Margaret said, "And take my heart with you."

The Duke of Suffolk said, "It is a jewel, locked to the most woeful casket that ever did contain a thing of worth.

"Just like a ship that has split in two, so we split up. This way I go and fall to death."

Queen Margaret said, "And this way I go and fall to death."

Cardinal Beaufort lay mortally ill and delirious in bed. By him were King Henry VI, the Earl of Salisbury, and the Earl of Warwick.

"How is my lord?" King Henry VI asked. "Speak, Cardinal Beaufort, to your sovereign."

Cardinal Beaufort replied, "If you are Death, I'll give you England's treasure, enough to purchase another such island, if you will let me live, and feel no pain."

King Henry VI said, "Ah, what a sign it is of evil life, where death's approach is seen as being so terrible!"

The Earl of Warwick said, "Beaufort, it is your sovereign who speaks to you."

Cardinal Beaufort said, "Bring me to my trial when you will. Didn't he — the Duke of Gloucester — die in his bed? Where else should he die? Can I make men live, whether they will or no?

"Oh, torture me no more! I will confess.

"Alive again? Then show me where he is. I'll give a thousand pounds to look at him.

"He has no eyes, the dust has blinded them. Comb down his hair. Look, look! It stands upright, like twigs smeared with birdlime — like a trap to catch my winged soul.

"Give me some drink; and tell the apothecary to bring the strong poison that I bought from him."

King Henry VI prayed, "Oh, Thou eternal Mover of the Heavens, look with a gentle eye upon this wretch! Oh, beat away the busy meddling fiend that lays strong siege to capture this wretch's soul. And, Thou eternal Mover of the Heavens, purge this black despair from his bosom!"

The Earl of Warwick said, "Look at how the pangs of death make him grin and bare his teeth!"

The Earl of Salisbury said, "Don't disturb him; let him pass peaceably."

King Henry VI said, "May he have peace to his soul, if that is God's good pleasure!

"Lord Cardinal Beaufort, if you are thinking about Heaven's bliss, hold up your hand; make a signal — a sign — of your hope."

Cardinal Beaufort died.

King Henry VI said, "He dies, and makes no sign. Oh, God, forgive him!"

"So bad a death is evidence of a monstrous life," the Earl of Warwick said.

"Forbear to judge, for we all are sinners," King Henry VI said. "God will be the judge.

"Close his eyes and draw closed the curtain around his bed; and let us all go to pray."

CHAPTER 4

— 4.1 —

Off the coast of Kent, a battle between two ships had taken place. The losing ship was the one carrying the disguised Duke of Suffolk as he attempted to sail to France. The Captain, a Master, a Master's-Mate, a man named Walter Whitmore, and others were meeting to decide what to do with the prisoners. Evening was falling. The Captain was the highest-ranking officer, while the Master was a high-ranking officer who was responsible for navigation.

The Captain said, "The showy, blabbing, and compassionate day has crept into the bosom of the sea, and now loud-howling wolves arouse the jades — dragons pulling the night-chariot — that drag the tragic melancholy night. These jades, with their drowsy, slow, and flagging wings, embrace dead men's graves and from their misty jaws breathe foul contagious darkness into the air."

Day is showy because it is bright with sunshine. It is blabbing because the daylight reveals what a criminal would prefer to be covered up by darkness, and it is compassionate because dirty — not-compassionate — deeds prefer to be done in the dark.

The Captain said, "Therefore bring forth the soldiers of our prize — the ship we captured. For, while our pinnace, aka small, light ship, anchors in the Downs, aka the sea off Kent's east coast, they shall make their ransom here on the sand, or stain and discolor with their blood this shore.

"Master, this prisoner freely I give to you, and you who are his Master's-Mate, take this second prisoner and make a profit from him. Walter Whitmore, this third prisoner is your share."

The first gentleman prisoner asked, "What is my ransom, Master? Let me know."

The Master replied, "A thousand crowns, or else lay down your head."

To lay down one's head was to be beheaded.

The Master's-Mate said to the second gentleman prisoner, "And so much shall you give, or off goes your head."

The Captain said to the two gentleman prisoners, "Do you think it too much to pay two thousand crowns, you who bear the name and bearing of gentlemen?"

Walter Whitmore advised, "Cut both the villains' throats."

He looked at his prisoner and said, "For die you shall."

He then said to the Captain and the other pirates, "Shall the lives of those whom we have lost in the fight be counterbalanced with such a petty sum!"

The first gentleman prisoner said, "I'll pay the ransom, sir; and therefore spare my life."

The second gentleman prisoner said, "And so will I, and I will write home for it immediately."

Walter Whitmore said to the third gentleman prisoner, who was the Duke of Suffolk in disguise, "I lost my eye in attacking the prize at close quarters, and therefore in order for me to get revenge for it, you shall die — and so would these other gentleman prisoners, if I might have my will."

The Captain advised, "Don't be so rash; take a ransom, and let him live."

The disguised Duke of Suffolk said, "Look at my George; I am a gentleman. Rate me at whatever you will; you shall be paid."

A George is a figure of St. George killing a dragon; it is part of the insignia of the Order of the Garter.

Walter Whitmore said, "And so I am and will be; the ransom I want is your life. My name is Walter Whitmore."

He pronounced "Walter" without the L: "Water." In this culture, this pronunciation was common.

Hearing this, and remembering the prophecy that he would die "by water," the Duke of Suffolk flinched, aka started.

Walter Whitmore said, "What! Why did you start? Does death frighten you?"

The Duke of Suffolk said, "Your name frightens me because in its sound is death. A cunning man who could foretell the future cast my horoscope and told me that by water I would die. Yet don't let this make you be bloody-minded. Your name is the medieval French Gaultier, if it were rightly pronounced."

"Gaultier or Walter, whichever it is, I don't care," Walter Whitmore said, "Never yet did base dishonor blur our name, but with our sword we wiped away the blot. Therefore, when merchant-like I sell my revenge by accepting a ransom, then let my sword be broken, my coat of arms be torn and defaced, and I be proclaimed a coward throughout the world!"

The Duke of Suffolk said, "Wait, Whitmore; for your prisoner is a Prince. I am the Duke of Suffolk, William de la Pole."

Walter Whitmore said, "The Duke of Suffolk muffled up in rags!"

The Duke of Suffolk replied, "Yes, but these rags are no part of the Duke. The Roman King of the gods, Jove, sometimes went disguised, and so why not I?"

Unfortunately for the Duke of Suffolk, he was greatly disliked by the people of England.

The Captain said, "But Jove was never slain, as you shall be."

Recognizing the Captain as a former servant of his, the Duke of Suffolk said, "You obscure and lowly yokel, King Henry VI's blood, the honorable blood of the House of Lancaster, must not be shed by such a jaded groom as you.

"Haven't you kissed your hand to show respect to me and haven't you held my stirrup?

"Haven't you bare-headed plodded by my mule as it wore a decorative cloth and thought yourself happy when I shook my head?

"How often have you waited at my cup, fed from my serving-dish, and kneeled down at the table when I have feasted with Queen Margaret?

"Remember it and let it make you crestfallen, yes, and abate your abhorrent and ill-timed pride.

"How often in our waiting-room lobby have you stood and duly waited for me to come forth?

"This hand of mine has written legal testimonials in your behalf, and therefore it shall charm your riotous tongue."

Such words were insulting, and they were spoken in an insulting voice.

Walter Whitmore said, "Speak, Captain, shall I stab this forlorn swain?"

"First let my words stab him, as he has me," the Captain said.

"Base, lowly born slave, your words are blunt and harmless and so are you," the Duke of Suffolk said.

The Captain said, "Convey him away from here and on our longboat's side strike off his head."

"You don't dare, for fear of losing your own head," the Duke of Suffolk, William de la Pole, said.

"Yes, I do dare, Pole," the Captain said.

"Pole!" the Duke of Suffolk said, outraged at not being addressed by his title. He regarded as an insult the Captain's addressing him by his family name.

In this culture, "Pole" was pronounced "Pool." The Captain made a series of insults, some of them punning on the name. The word "poll" means "head." The head of a beheaded man was displayed on a pole. "Sir Pol" was a common name for a parrot. A kennel is an open gutter. A sink is a cesspool.

The Captain said, "Pool! Sir Pool! Lord! Yes, kennel, puddle, sink — whose filth and dirt muddies the silver spring where England drinks.

"Now I will dam up your gaping, greedy mouth because it swallowed the treasure of the realm.

"Your lips that kissed the Queen shall sweep the ground.

"And you who smiled at good Duke Humphrey of Gloucester's death shall grin in vain against the unfeeling winds."

The Duke of Suffolk's head would be displayed on a pole in a place open to the weather.

The Captain continued, "These winds in contempt shall hiss at you again, and you shall be wedded to the hags of Hell — the Furies — because you dared to betroth a mighty lord — Henry VI — to the daughter of a worthless King — Reignier — who lacks subjects, wealth, and a diadem.

"By means of Devilish and cunning political intrigue, you have grown great, and, like ambitious Sulla, you have gorged yourself with gobbets — pieces of raw flesh — of your mother country's bleeding heart."

Lucius Cornelius Sulla was a Roman General who used his power as Dictator of Rome to kill his enemies.

The Captain continued, "Anjou and Maine were sold to France by you.

"Because of you, the false revolting Normans disdain to call us lord, and the citizens of Picardy have slain their governors, surprised our forts, and sent the ragged soldiers wounded home.

"The Princely Warwick, and all the Nevilles, whose dreadful swords were never drawn in vain, are rising up in arms because they hate you, and now the House of York, thrust from the crown by the shameful murder of the guiltless King Richard II and by lofty proud encroaching tyranny, burns with revenging fire. Their hopeful colors, aka battle flags, raise our half-faced Sun — a Sun bursting through clouds, aka the symbol of Richard II — striving to shine, under which is written '*Invitis nubibus*.'"

The Latin "*Invitis nubibus*" means "Despite the clouds."

The Captain continued, "The commoners here in Kent are up in arms.

"And, to conclude, reproach and beggary have crept into the palace of our King Henry VI, and all because of you.

"Take him away! Take him to his death!"

The Duke of Suffolk said, "Oh, I wish that I were a god, to shoot forth thunder upon these paltry, servile, abject drudges! Small things make basely born men proud: This villain here, who is the Captain of a mere pinnace, threatens more than Bargulus, the strong Illyrian pirate.

"Drones don't suck the blood of eagles, but they do rob beehives. It is impossible that I should die by such a lowly vassal as yourself. Your words move rage and not remorse in me.

"I am carrying a message from Queen Margaret to the King of France. I order you to waft — transport by water — me safely across the Channel."

The Captain said, "Walter —"

Knowing what the Captain was going to order him to do, Walter Whitmore said, "Come, Suffolk, I must waft you to your death."

He was identifying himself with Chiron, the mythological figure who ferried souls to the Land of the Dead.

The Duke of Suffolk said, "*Gelidus timor occupat artus*. It is you I fear."

"*Gelidus timor occupat artus*" is Latin for "Cold fear seizes my limbs."

Walter Whitmore said, "You shall have reason to fear before I leave you. Are you daunted now? Now will you stoop to me?"

The first gentleman prisoner said, "My gracious lord, beg him for your life. Speak respectfully to him."

The Duke of Suffolk replied, "Suffolk's imperial tongue is stern and rough, used to command, untaught to plead for favor."

Using the royal plural, he said, "Far be it that we should honor such as these with humble entreaties. No, I would rather let my head stoop to the chopping block than let these knees bow to anyone except to the God of Heaven and to my King. And I would sooner have my chopped-off head dance upon a bloody pole than stand uncovered — with my hand holding my hat in respect — to honor the vulgar groom, aka servant.

"True nobility is exempt from fear. I can bear more than you dare execute."

The Captain ordered, "Haul him away, and let him talk no more."

The Duke of Suffolk said, "Come, soldiers, show me what cruelty you can, so that this my death may never be forgotten!

"Great men often die at the hands of vile scoundrels.

"A Roman sword-fighter and outlaw slave murdered sweet Marcus Tullius Cicero, the great Roman orator.

"Brutus' bastard hand stabbed Julius Caesar.

"Savage islanders murdered Pompey the Great.

"And now Suffolk dies at the hands of pirates."

The Duke of Suffolk's education was lacking. Cicero was killed by two of Marcus Antony's soldiers: a centurion named Herennius and a tribune named Pompilius Laena. Brutus was incorrectly thought to be Julius Caesar's bastard son. Pompey was killed by some of his former centurions on the coast of Egypt.

Centurions and tribunes are commanders of the ancient Roman army.

Walter Whitmore and others took the Duke of Suffolk away to be killed.

The Captain said, "And as for these whose ransom we have set, it is our pleasure that one of them depart.

"Therefore come you with us and let him" — he pointed to the first gentleman prisoner — "go."

Everyone exited except for the first gentleman prisoner.

Walter Whitmore returned, carrying the Duke of Suffolk's head and body.

He threw them on the ground and said, "There let his head and lifeless body lie, until the Queen his mistress bury them."

The first gentleman prisoner said, "Oh, barbarous and bloody spectacle! I will carry his corpse to the King. If he doesn't revenge this death, his friends will. So will the Queen, who regarded him dearly when he was alive."

He carried away the head and body.

At Blackheath, Kent, two people named George Bevis and John Holland talked together. They were carrying staves — wooden boards, and they were waiting for Jack Cade and his rebels to arrive.

George Bevis said, "Come, and get yourself a sword, although it is made of thin wood. The rebels have been up these past two days."

George Bevis meant "up in arms," but Holland pretended he meant "up and out of bed."

Holland said, "They have the more need to sleep now, then."

George Bevis said, "I tell you, Jack Cade the clothier means to dress the commonwealth, and turn it, and set a new nap upon it."

A clothier makes woolen cloth. George Bevis was saying that Jack Cade was going to reform the commonwealth the way that a tailor could make old clothing seem new: turn it inside out, and give it a new surface, aka nap.

"He needs to do that, for the commonwealth is threadbare," Holland said. "Well, I say it was never a merry world in England since gentlemen rose in rank and power."

"Oh, what a miserable age!" George Bevis said. "Virtue is not regarded in handicraftsmen. We skilled workers are not valued."

"The nobility think it is degrading to wear leather aprons," Holland said.

"What's more, the King's Council are not good workmen," George Bevis said.

"True," Holland said, "and yet it is said, labor in your vocation, which is as much to say as, let the magistrates be laboring men; and therefore we laboring men should be magistrates."

"You have hit the target," George Bevis said, "for there's no better sign of a fine, splendid mind than a hard, calloused hand."

Seeing the rebels approaching, Holland said, "I see them! I see them! There's the son of Best, the tanner of Wingham —"

"He shall have the skin of our enemies, to make dog's-leather of," George Bevis said.

Dog's-leather was dogskin, a kind of leather used to make gloves.

"And there's Dick the Butcher —" Holland said.

"Then is sin struck down like an ox, and iniquity's throat cut like a calf,"
George Bevis said.

"And there's Smith the Weaver —" Holland said.

"*Argo*, their thread of life is spun," George Bevis said.

"*Argo*" was an uneducated person's way of saying "*Ergo*," which is Latin for
"Therefore."

"Come, come, let's fall in with them," Holland said.

Jack Cade, Dick the Butcher, Smith the Weaver, a sawyer — a person who
saws wood — and many other rebels arrived.

Using the royal plural, Jack Cade said, "We, John Cade, so named for our
supposed father —"

Dick the Butcher and the other rebels knew who Jack Cade was. He was a
man just like them, a rebel who was not royalty, although he was pretending to
be royalty — and he and they knew that he was pretending.

Dick the Butcher said, "Or rather, so named for stealing a cade of herrings."

A "cade" is a barrel.

Jack Cade said, "For our enemies shall fall before us, inspired with the spirit
of putting down Kings and Princes.

He then ordered, "Command silence."

Dick the Butcher shouted, "Silence!"

Jack Cade said, "My father was a Mortimer —"

Mortimer was supposed to have a better claim to the throne than King
Henry VI, but Jack Cade's father was a mortarer, a person who laid bricks. Jack
Cade's father was not a Mortimer.

Dick the Butcher said, "He was an honest man, and a good bricklayer."

Jack Cade said, "My mother was a Plantagenet —"

A "jennet" is a lance, so his mother was a woman who knew about planting
a particular phallic-shaped object, an act that sometimes results in the
production of babies when an actual phallus is used.

Dick the Butcher said, "I knew her well; she was a midwife."

Jack Cade said, "My wife was descended from the family known as the
Lacies —"

Dick the Butcher said, "She was, indeed, a peddler's daughter, and sold
many laces."

Smith the Weaver said, "But now of late, not able to travel with her furred pack, she washes bucks here at home."

A "furred pack" is a peddler's pack with the fur on the outside. To "wash bucks" meant to wash loads of soiled clothing. " The word "buck" means "laundry."

Smith the Weaver's words had a bawdy sense. To "travel with a furred pack" meant to "labor as a prostitute." A "pack" is a container, and a "furred pack" is a vulva (including the opening of the vagina) with pubic hair; a vagina can be a container for a penis. A "buck" is a strapping young man, and to "wash bucks" means to get them — that is, a certain part of their body — wet.

Jack Cade said, "Therefore I am of an honorable house."

Dick the Butcher said, "Yes, by my faith, the field is honorable, and there was he born, under a hedge, because his father never had a house except the cage."

The "cage" is a prison for petty criminals.

"Valiant I am," Jack Cade said.

Smith the Weaver said, "He must needs be valiant; for beggary is valiant."

"Valiant beggars" were able-bodied beggars; it was against the law to give alms to them. The penalty for able-bodied people who were caught begging was a whipping.

Jack Cade said, "I am able to endure much."

Dick the Butcher said, "There is no question about that; for I have seen him whipped three market-days without intermission."

"I fear neither sword nor fire," Jack Cade said.

Smith the Weaver said, "He need not fear the sword; for his coat is of proof. His coat has had so much liquor spilled on it that it is obvious that Jack Cade is always too drunk to fear anything."

Dick the Butcher said, "But I think he should stand in fear of fire because he was burnt on the hand for the stealing of sheep. His hand was branded with a 'T' for 'Thief.'"

Jack Cade said, "Be brave, then; for your captain is brave, and vows reformation of the commonwealth. There shall be in England seven halfpenny loaves sold for a penny — you will get more bread for your money. The three-hooped pot shall have ten hoops — you shall get more beer. I will make it a felony to drink small beer; instead of small beer, which is weak, you shall drink strong beer. All the realm shall be common property. In Cheapside — London's main market area — my horse shall go to eat grass, and when I am King, as King I will be —"

All the rebels present shouted, "God save your majesty!"

"I thank you, good people," Jack Cade said. "There shall be no money; all shall eat and drink at my expense, and I will clothe them all in one livery so that they may agree like brothers and worship me their lord."

Dick the Butcher said, "The first thing we do, let's kill all the lawyers."

Jack Cade said, "I intend to do that. Isn't this a lamentable thing, that the skin of an innocent lamb should be made into parchment, which, being scribbled over, should undo and ruin a man? Some say the bee stings, but I say that it is the bee's wax that is used to seal legal documents that stings because I signed and sealed a legal document only once, and I have never been my own man since."

He heard a noise and said, "What's happening! Who's there?"

Some rebels came forward, bringing with them a prisoner: the Clerk of Chatham. Clerks were learned men who could read, write, and do arithmetic. Clerks were also often schoolteachers.

Smith the Weaver said, "This is the Clerk of Chatham: He can write and read and do arithmetic."

"Oh, monstrous!" Jack Cade said.

Smith the Weaver said, "We captured him while he was preparing samples of handwriting for schoolboys to copy."

"Here's a villain!" Jack Cade said.

Smith the Weaver said, "He has a book in his pocket with red letters in it."

Almanacs, which were consulted by astrologers, had certain dates printed in red. Schoolbooks had capital letters printed in red.

Jack Cade said, "So then he is a conjurer."

Dick the Butcher said, "He can make obligations, aka bonds, and write court-handwriting, which is used for legal documents."

"I am sorry to hear it," Jack Cade said. "The man is a proper man, a good-looking man, on my honor; unless I find him guilty, he shall not die.

"Come here, sirrah, I must examine you. What is your name?"

"Sirrah" was used to address a person of lower social standing than the speaker.

The Clerk replied, "Emmanuel."

Dick the Butcher said, "They write 'Emmanuel' on the top of letters. It will go hard with you."

Emmanuel is a Hebrew word that means "God is with us."

"Don't interrupt me," Jack Cade said.

Then he asked the Clerk, "Do you write your name? Or do you sign your name with a mark, like an honest plain-dealing man?"

The Clerk said, "Sir, I thank God that I have been so well brought up that I can write my name."

The rebels shouted, "He has confessed. Away with him! He's a villain and a traitor."

"Away with him, I say!" Jack Cade shouted. "Hang him with his pen and inkhorn about his neck."

The inkhorn was used to hold ink for writing.

A rebel took the Clerk away.

A rebel named Michael arrived and asked, "Where's our General?"

Jack Cade replied, "Here I am, you particular fellow."

"Flee, flee, flee!" Michael said. "Sir Humphrey Stafford and his brother are close by, with the King's forces."

"Stand, villain, stand, or I'll fell you down," Jack Cade said. "He shall be encountered with a man as good as himself. He is only a knight, isn't he?"

Michael replied, "He is no better."

Jack Cade said, "To equal him, I will make myself a knight right now."

He knelt and then said, "Rise up, Sir John Mortimer."

He stood up and said, "Now let me at him!"

Sir Humphrey Stafford and William Stafford arrived, along with a drummer and some soldiers.

Sir Humphrey Stafford said to the rebels, "Rebellious peasants, the filth and scum of Kent, marked from birth for the gallows, lay your weapons down; go home to your cottages, forsake this servant named Jack Cade. The King is merciful, if you revolt against Jack Cade and again swear allegiance to your King."

William Stafford said, "But the King will be angry, wrathful, and inclined to blood, if you go forward and continue to rebel against him; therefore yield, or die."

Jack Cade said, "As for these silken-coated slaves, the Staffords, I care not. It is to you, good people, whom I speak, and over whom, in time to come, I hope to reign, for I am the rightful heir to the crown."

Sir Humphrey Stafford said, "Villain, your father was a plasterer, and you yourself are a shearman, aren't you?"

A shearman cuts off the extra nap from wool cloth.

Jack Cade said, "And Adam was a gardener."

A proverb stated, "When Adam delved and Eve span, / Who was then the gentleman?"

Adam and Eve were the first human beings. After being cast out of the Garden of Eden, they had to work in order to survive.

To "delve" is to plow. "Span" is the past tense of "spin." Spinning is part of the process of making cloth.

William Stafford asked, "And what of that?"

Jack Cade replied, "By the Virgin Mary, this: Edmund Mortimer, Earl of March, married the Duke of Clarence's daughter, didn't he?"

Sir Humphrey Stafford replied, "Yes, sir."

"By her he had two children at one birth," Jack Cade said.

"That's false," William Stafford said.

"There's the question," Jack Cade said, "but I say that it is true. The elder of them, being put to nurse, was by a beggar-woman stolen away, and, ignorant of his birth and parentage, he became a bricklayer when he came to age. I am his son. Deny it, if you can."

Dick the Butcher said, "It is very true; therefore, he shall be King."

Smith the Weaver said, "Sir, he made a chimney in my father's house, and the bricks are alive at this day to testify to it; therefore, don't deny it."

Sir Humphrey Stafford said, "And will you credit the words of this base drudge, who doesn't know what he is saying?"

The rebels said, "By the Virgin Mary, we will; therefore, get you gone. Leave."

William Stafford said, "Jack Cade, the Duke of York has taught you to say this."

Jack Cade said quietly so only the rebels could hear, "He lies, for I invented it myself."

He then said out loud, "Bah, sirrah, tell the King from me that for the sake of his father, King Henry V, in whose time boys went to span-counter for French crowns, I am content that he shall reign, but I'll be Lord Protector over him."

King Henry V won many notable victories over the French. The English and the French fought man to man.

Span-counter is a game in which boys throw counters with the object of throwing their counter close to — within a hand-span — of the other boy's counter.

Dick the Butcher said, "And furthermore, we'll have the Lord Say's head for selling the Dukedom of Maine."

Jack Cade said, "And for good reason; for thereby is England mained — I mean, maimed — and obliged to go about with a staff, except that my power holds it up."

He said to the rebels, "Fellow Kings, I tell you that the Lord Say has gelded the commonwealth, and made it a eunuch, and more than that, he can speak French, and therefore he is a traitor."

Sir Humphrey Stafford said, "Oh, gross and miserable ignorance!"

Jack Cade said, "Answer this, if you can: The Frenchmen are our enemies. And so, then, I ask only this: Can he who speaks with the tongue of an enemy be a good counselor, or not?"

The rebels shouted, "He cannot, and therefore we'll have his head."

William Stafford said to his brother, "Well, seeing that gentle words will not prevail, assail them with the army of the King."

Sir Humphrey Stafford ordered, "Herald, go; and throughout every town proclaim to be traitors those who are up in arms with Jack Cade so that those who flee before the battle ends may, even in their wives' and children's sight, be hanged up at their doors as an example to others.

"Those of you who are the King's friends, follow me."

Sir Humphrey Stafford and William Stafford exited with their drummer and soldiers.

Jack Cade said to the rebels, "And you who love the commoners, follow me. Now show yourselves to be men; it is for liberty. We will not leave one lord, one gentleman, alive. Spare none except such men as go about in shoes with hobnails, for they are thrifty and honest men, and such as would, except that they dare not, take our parts."

Dick the Butcher said, "They are all in order and march toward us. They are drawn up in military formation."

Jack Cade said, "But then we are in order when we are most out of order."

He and the rebels were most in order — in military formation — when they were most out of order — rebelling against the King.

Jack Cade ordered, "Come, march forward."

The battle took place, and Sir Humphrey Stafford and William Stafford were slain. Jack Cade and the rebels then discussed their victory.

Jack Cade asked, "Where's Dick, the butcher of Ashford?"

Dick the Butcher said, "Here, sir."

"They fell before you like sheep and oxen, and you behaved yourself as if you were in your own slaughterhouse; therefore, I will reward you thus: Lent shall be twice as long as it is now, and you shall have a license to kill for a hundred lacking one."

During Lent, people did not eat meat unless they were invalids. Special licenses were granted to butchers to kill animals for food during Lent. Many licenses were granted for 99 years. However, Jack Cade was ambiguous. He could have meant that Dick the Butcher could kill 99 animals or that he could kill as many animals as would feed 99 people.

"I desire no more," Dick the Butcher said.

Jack Cade said, "And, to speak the truth, you deserve no less."

He pointed to Sir Humphrey Stafford's helmet and armor and said, "This memorial of the victory I will wear, and the bodies of the Staffords shall be dragged at my horse's heels until I come to London, where we will have the Mayor's sword borne before us."

Dick the Butcher said, "If we mean to thrive and do good, break open the jails and let out the prisoners."

"Don't worry about that — I promise I will do that," Jack Cade said. "Come, let's march towards London."

In the King's palace in London, several people were meeting: King Henry VI, Queen Margaret, the Duke of Buckingham, and Lord Say.

The King was holding a document sent to him from Jack Cade. Queen Margaret was holding the Duke of Suffolk's severed head.

Queen Margaret said, "Often I have heard that grief softens the mind and makes it fearful and degenerate. Think therefore on revenge and cease to weep. But who can cease to weep while looking at this head? Here may his head lie on my throbbing breast, but where's the body that I would embrace?"

The Duke of Buckingham asked, "What answer does your grace make to the rebels' written petition?"

King Henry VI said, "I'll send some holy bishop to entreat them to be peaceful, for God forbid that so many simple souls should perish by the sword! And I myself, rather than allow bloody war to cut them short, will parley with Jack Cade, their General. But wait, I'll read the written petition over once again."

Still holding the Duke of Suffolk's head, Queen Margaret said, "Ah, barbarous villains! Has this lovely face ruled, like a wandering planet, over me, and could it not force them to relent, who were unworthy to behold the same face?"

Astrologers believed that the planets, which wandered the night sky, unlike the fixed stars, ruled human destiny.

King Henry VI said, "Lord Say, Jack Cade has sworn to have your head."

"Yes, but I hope your highness shall have his," Lord Say replied.

"What is this, madam!" King Henry VI said to Queen Margaret. "Still lamenting and mourning for Suffolk's death? I am afraid, love, if I were the one who is dead, you would not mourn so much for me."

Queen Margaret replied, "No, my love. I would not mourn, but die for you."

A messenger entered the room.

King Henry VI said, "What is it? What's the news? Why have you come in such haste?"

"The rebels are in Southwark, just south of the Thames River. They will soon cross London Bridge," the messenger said. "Flee, my lord! Jack Cade proclaims himself Lord Mortimer, descended from the Duke of Clarence's house, and he calls your grace a usurper openly and vows to crown himself in Westminster.

"His army is a ragged multitude of rustics and peasants, uncivilized and merciless. The deaths of Sir Humphrey Stafford and his brother have given them heart and courage to proceed. They call all scholars, lawyers, courtiers, and gentlemen traitorous parasites, and they intend to kill them."

"Oh, graceless men!" King Henry VI said. "They lack the grace of God, and they know not what they do."

Luke 23:34 states, "*Then said Jesus, Father, forgive them; for they know not what they do. And they parted his raiment, and cast lots*" (King James Version).

The Duke of Buckingham said, "My gracious lord, return to Kenilworth, near Warwick, until an army is raised to put them down."

Queen Margaret said, "Ah, if the Duke of Suffolk were now alive, these Kentish rebels would be soon subdued!"

"Lord Say, the traitors hate you," King Henry VI said. "Therefore, go away with us to Kenilworth."

Lord Say replied, "If I go with you, then your grace's person might be in danger. The sight of me is odious in their eyes, and in seeking to harm me, the rebels may harm you. Therefore, in this city I will stay and live alone as secretly as I may."

Another messenger arrived and said, "Jack Cade has captured London Bridge. The citizens flee and forsake their houses. The rascal people, thirsting after prey, join with the traitor, and they jointly swear to despoil and plunder the city and your royal court."

The Duke of Buckingham advised the King, "Don't linger, my lord. Go away, and take to horse."

"Come, Margaret," King Henry VI said. "God, our hope, will succor us."

Queen Margaret replied, "My hope is gone, now that the Duke of Suffolk is deceased."

King Henry VI said to Lord Say, "Farewell, my lord. Don't trust the Kentish rebels."

"Trust nobody, for fear you will be betrayed," the Duke of Buckingham advised.

Lord Say said, "The trust I have is in my innocence, and therefore I am bold and resolute."

— 4.5 —

A commander named Lord Scales walked on top of a wall of the Tower of London, which King Henry VI had ordered him to defend. Two or three citizens arrived and stood below him on the ground.

Lord Scales saw them and asked, "What's happening? Has Jack Cade been slain?"

"No, my lord," the first citizen said. "Nor is he likely to be slain, for the rebels have captured London Bridge, killing all those who stood against them. The Lord Mayor begs your honor for aid from the Tower of London to defend the city from the rebels."

"Such aid as I can spare, you shall command," Lord Scales said, "but I am troubled here with the rebels myself. The rebels have attempted to capture the Tower of London. But go to Smithfield and gather troops, and thither I will send you the great warrior Matthew Goffe.

"Fight for your King, your country, and your lives. And so, farewell, for I must go away from here again."

— 4.6 —

On Cannon Street in London, Jack Cade and other rebels, including Dick the Butcher and Smith the Weaver, stood. Jack Cade struck his staff on London Stone, a historical landmark that is thought to be a remnant of London's Roman history.

Jack Cade said, "Now I, Mortimer, am lord of this city. And here, sitting upon London Stone, I order and command that, at the city's cost, the Pissing Conduit run nothing but claret wine this first year of our reign."

The Pissing Conduit was a source of water for London's poor.

Jack Cade continued, "And from now henceforward it shall be treason for anyone who calls me anything other than Lord Mortimer."

A soldier came running and shouted, "Jack Cade! Jack Cade!"

Jack Cade said, "Knock him down there."

His supporters killed the soldier.

Smith the Weaver said, "If this fellow is wise, he'll never call you Jack Cade again. I think he has had a very fair warning."

Dick the Butcher said, "My lord, there's an army gathered together in Smithfield."

Jack Cade said, "Come, then, let's go fight with them, but first, go and set London Bridge on fire, and if you can, burn down the Tower of London, too. Come, let's go."

In Smithfield, London, the battle had taken place. The rebels were victorious and had killed the great warrior Matthew Goffe.

Jack Cade said, "So, sirs, now some of you go and pull down the Savoy — the residence of the Duke of Lancaster. Others of you go to the Inns of Court — the London law schools and the place where London lawyers work and reside. Down with them all!"

Dick the Butcher said, "I have a suit — a formal request — for your lordship."

Jack Cade replied, "If you want a lordship, you shall have it for calling me 'my lordship.'"

Dick the Butcher said, "I request only that the laws of England may come out of your mouth."

John Holland said, "By the Mass, it will be sore — poor and painful — law, then, for he was thrust in the mouth with a spear, and the wound has not healed yet."

Smith the Weaver said, "John, it will be stinking law because his breath stinks from eating toasted cheese."

Jack Cade replied to Dick the Butcher, "I have thought about it, and it shall be so. All laws will come from my mouth. Leave, and burn all the records of the realm. My mouth shall be the Parliament of England."

John Holland said, "Then we are likely to have biting — severe — statutes, unless his teeth are pulled out."

Jack Cade said, "And henceforward all things shall belong to the whole community — they shall be owned in common."

A messenger arrived and said, "My lord, a prize, a prize! Here's the Lord Say, who sold the towns in France; he is the man who made us pay one and twenty fifteens, and one shilling to the pound, the last subsidy."

The messenger was exaggerating how much taxes the commoners paid. One and twenty fifteens totaled 140 percent.

Jack Cade said, "Well, he shall be beheaded for it ten times."

Lord Say, guarded by the rebel George Bevis, arrived.

Jack Cade then said to Lord Say, "Ah, you say, you serge — no, you buckram lord!"

"Say" was a fine-textured cloth, "serge" was a woolen cloth, and "buckram" was a cloth that was stiffened with glue.

Jack Cade continued, "Now you are within point-blank range of our regal jurisdiction. What can you answer to my majesty for the giving up of Normandy to Mounsieur Basimecu, the Dauphin of France?"

"Mounsieur" was an uneducated pronunciation of the French "*Monsieur,*" and "Basimecu" was an uneducated pronunciation of the French "*Baise mon cul,*" aka "F**k my *ss."

Jack Cade continued, "Be it known to you by these presence, even the presence of Lord Mortimer, that I am the besom — broom — that must sweep the court clean of such filth as you are. "

He was confusing the Latin "*per has literas presents,*" aka "by these present documents," and "in this presence."

Jack Cade continued, "You have most traitorously corrupted the youth of the realm by erecting a grammar school, and whereas our forefathers previously had no other books but the score and the tally, which are a way of recording debts, you have caused printing to be used, and, contrary to the King, his crown, and his dignity, you have built a paper mill."

The ancient Greek philosopher Socrates taught the youth of Athens, for which activity he was accused in a lawsuit of "corrupting the youth of Athens."

Jack Cade continued, "It will be proved to your face that you have men about you who usually talk of a noun and a verb, and these are such abominable words as no Christian ear can endure to hear. You have appointed justices of peace to call poor men before them about matters they were not able to answer satisfactorily. Moreover, you have put them in prison, and because they could not read, you have hanged them; when, indeed, for just that reason they have been most worthy to live."

In this culture, priests were exempt from being tried in a criminal court, although they could be tried in an ecclesiastical court. Priests were able to read Latin and anyone who could prove that he could read Latin could avoid a sentence of capital punishment given in a criminal court by claiming benefit of clergy.

Jack Cade continued, "You ride in a footcloth, don't you?"

He meant that Lord Say rode a horse that was decorated with a footcloth
— a richly ornamented cloth that was draped over the horse's back.

"What of that?" Lord Say asked.

Jack Cade said, "By the Virgin Mary, you ought not to let your horse wear
a cloak, when men who are more honest than you go about in their tights and
jackets."

Dick the Butcher added, "And work in their shirt, too, as for example I
myself, who am a butcher, do."

Jack Cade's point was that animals ought not to be better dressed than
human beings.

Lord Say began, "You men of Kent —"

Dick the Butcher interrupted, "What do you say about Kent?"

Knowing that the rebels did not know Latin, Lord Say replied, "Nothing
but this: It is '*bona terra, mala gens.*'"

"*Bona terra, mala gens*" is Latin for "a good land, a bad people."

"Away with him, away with him!" Jack Cade said, "He speaks Latin."

Lord Say said, "Hear me speak, and then take me where you will.

"Julius Caesar, in his *Commentaries on the Gallic War*, wrote that Kent is
the most civil place of this isle. Sweet is the country, because full of riches. The
people are liberal, valiant, active, and wealthy, which makes me hope you are
not devoid of pity.

"I did not sell Maine, I did not lose Normandy, yet I am willing to lose my
life to recover them.

"As a judge, I have always given justice with mercy. Prayers and tears have
moved me, but gifts never could. I did not accept bribes.

"When have I exacted any tax at your hands, except in order to maintain
the King, the realm, and you?

"I have bestowed large gifts on learned clerks because my education
preferred me to the King. Seeing that ignorance is the curse of God, while
knowledge is the wing wherewith we fly to Heaven, unless you are possessed
with Devilish spirits, you cannot but refrain from murdering me.

"This tongue has parleyed with foreign Kings for your benefit —"

Jack Cade said, "Tut, when have you struck even one blow on the
battlefield?"

Lord Say said, "Great men have hands that reach far. Often have I struck those whom I never saw and struck them dead."

George Bevis said, "Oh, monstrous coward! To come up behind folks and then strike them dead!"

Lord Say said, "These cheeks of mine are pale because I spent so much time watching out for your good."

Jack Cade said, "Give him a box on the ear and that will make his cheeks red again."

Lord Say said, "Long sitting as a judge to rule in poor men's law cases has made me full of sickness and diseases."

Jack Cade said, "You shall have a hempen caudle, then, and the help of hatchet."

A caudle is a warm drink intended to restore invalids to health. A hempen caudle is a hangman's noose. The word "hatchet" refers to an executioner's ax. After being hung and then beheaded so that one's head can be displayed on a pole, no one has to worry about sickness and disease.

Dick the Butcher asked Lord Say, who was trembling, "Why are you quivering, man?"

"The palsy, and not fear, affects me, an old man, and makes me tremble," Lord Say replied.

Jack Cade said, "He nods at us, as if to say, 'I'll get even with you.' I'll see if his head will stand steadier on a pole, or not. Take him away, and behead him."

Lord Say said, "Tell me in what I have offended most? Have I sought wealth or honors? Tell me. Are my chests filled up with gold that I have extorted from others? Is my apparel sumptuous to behold? Whom have I injured with the result that you seek my death? These hands are free from the shedding of guiltless blood. This breast is free of harboring foul deceitful thoughts. Oh, let me live!"

John Cade thought, *I feel remorse in myself because of his words, but I'll bridle my remorse. He shall die, even if it be only for pleading so well for his life.*

He said out loud, "Away with him! He has a familiar spirit under his tongue; he speaks not in God's name."

Witches had familiars — spirits that served them.

Jack Cade continued, "Go, take him away, I say, and strike off his head immediately; and then break into the house of his son-in-law, Sir James Cromer, and strike off his head, and bring both heads on two poles here."

The rebels said, "It shall be done."

"Ah, countrymen!" Lord Say said. "If when you make your prayers, God would be so obdurate as yourselves, how would it fare with your departed souls? Therefore relent now, and save my life."

Jack Cade ordered, "Take him away! And do as I command you."

Some rebels, including Dick the Butcher, exited with Lord Say.

Jack Cade said, "The proudest peer in the realm shall not wear a head on his shoulders, unless he pays me tribute. Not a maid shall be married, but she shall pay to me her maidenhead before her husband can have it. Men shall hold land from me *in capite*."

"*In capite*" was a Latin phrase meaning "from the head." The Latin legal phrase referred to land held directly from the King, who was the head of the country.

Jack Cade continued, "And we order and command that husbands' wives be as free and sexually available as heart can wish or tongue can tell — you will get as much sex as you could want or ask for."

A rebel arrived and said, "Captain, London Bridge is on fire!"

Jack Cade said, "Run to Billingsgate and fetch pitch and flax and quench it."

Pitch and flax would make the fire burn more fiercely.

Dick the Butcher and a Sergeant arrived.

The Sergeant said, "Justice, justice, I ask you for justice, sir. Let me have justice on this fellow Dick the Butcher here."

Jack Cade asked, "Why? What has he done?"

"Sir, he has raped my wife," the Sergeant said.

Dick the Butcher said to Jack Cade, "Why, my lord, he would have arrested me and so I went and entered my action in his wife's proper house."

"Arrested" also meant "stopped."

"Entered my action in his wife's proper house" meant 1) "stated my law case in his wife's house," and 2) "entered my penis and its action in his wife's body."

Jack Cade said, "Dick, follow your suit in her common place."

This meant 1) "Dick, pursue your law case in her common meetinghouse," and 2) "Dick, pursue your sexual desire in her vagina, which is open to all."

John Cade then said to the Sergeant, "You whoreson villain, you are a Sergeant — you'll take any man by the throat for twelve pence, and arrest a man when he's at dinner, and have him in prison before the food is out of his mouth."

He then said to Dick the Butcher, "Go, Dick, take him away from here. Cut out his tongue for deception, cripple him for running, and, to conclude, brain him with his own mace."

Dick the Butcher took the Sergeant away.

A rebel asked Jack Cade, "My lord, when shall we go to Cheapside and take up commodities upon our bills?"

"Take up commodities upon our bills" meant 1) "Buy goods [commodities] on credit [bills]," 2) "Take women's sexual organs [commodities] upon our penises [bills]," aka rape women, and 3) "Steal [Take] goods [commodities] by using our bills [long-handled weapons with blades]."

Jack Cade said, "By the Virgin Mary, right away. He who will lustily stand to it shall go with me and take up these commodities following — item, a gown, a kirtle [outer petticoat], a petticoat, and a smock [ladies' undergarment]."

"Stand to it" meant "get an erection."

The rebels shouted, "Oh, splendid!"

Two rebels arrived, carrying Lord Say's head and Sir James Cromer's head on two poles.

Jack Cade said, "But isn't this more splendid? Let them kiss one another, for they loved each other well when they were alive."

The two rebels holding the poles brought the heads together as if the heads were kissing.

Jack Cade continued, "Now part them again, lest they consult about the giving up of some more towns in France.

"Soldiers, defer the despoiling and plundering of the city until night, for with these heads borne before us, instead of maces — staffs of office — we will ride through the streets, and at every corner we will have them kiss. Away! Let's go!"

<h1 style="text-align:center">— 4.8 —</h1>

A battle was being fought at Southwark, a district of London.

Jack Cade ordered, "Up Fish Street! Down Saint Magnus' Corner! Kill and knock down! Throw them into the Thames River!"

Fish Street was a major approach to London Bridge. Saint Magnus' Corner was at the lower end of Fish Street and the place where Saint Magnus' Church stood.

A parley sounded. The Duke of Buckingham and Lord Clifford, who were representatives of King Henry VI, wished to talk to the rebels.

"What noise is this I hear?" Jack Cade said. "Does anyone dare to be so bold to sound either a retreat or a parley, when I command them to kill?"

The Duke of Buckingham and Lord Clifford arrived with many soldiers.

The Duke of Buckingham, who had heard Jack Cade's second question, replied, "Yes, here are those who dare and will disturb you.

"Know, Cade, we come as ambassadors from the King to the commoners whom you have misled, and here we officially declare free pardon to all who will forsake you and go home in peace."

Lord Clifford said, "What do you say, countrymen? Will you relent, and will you yield to mercy while it is offered to you? Or will you let a rebel lead you to your deaths?

"Whoever loves the King and will embrace his pardon, let him fling up his cap and cry, 'God save his majesty!'

"Whoever hates the King and does not honor his father, Henry V, who made all France quake, let him shake his weapon defiantly at us and pass by."

All of the rebels except Jack Cade flung their caps up in the air and cried, "God save the King! God save the King!"

Jack Cade said, "Buckingham and Clifford, are you so daring? And you, base peasants, do you believe him? Will you have to be hanged with your worthless pardons about your necks? Has my sword broken through London gates so that you would leave me at the White Hart Inn where I am residing in Southwark? I thought you would never have surrendered these weapons until you had recovered your ancient freedom, but you are all recreants and despicable people, and you delight to live in slavery to the nobility.

"Let them break your backs with burdens, take your houses over your heads, and rape your wives and daughters in front of your faces. As for me, I will look out for myself, and so may God's curse fall upon you all!"

All of the rebels shouted, "We'll follow Cade! We'll follow Cade!"

Lord Clifford asked, "Is Cade the son of Henry V? Is that why you exclaim you'll go with him? Will he conduct you through the heart of France, and make the lowest born of you Earls and Dukes?

"Alas, he has no home, no place to fly to, nor does he know how to live except by pillaging, unless he makes his living by robbing your friends and us.

"Wouldn't it be a shame, if while you live as rebels, the fearsome French, whom you recently vanquished, would make a start over seas and vanquish you? I think already in this civil broil I see them lording it in London streets, crying 'Villiago!' — 'Villain!' — at all whom they meet.

"It is better that ten thousand lowly born Cades die than that you should kneel to a Frenchman's mercy.

"Go to France, go to France, and get what you have lost. Spare England, for it is your native coast. King Henry VI has money, you are strong and manly, and God is on our side, so don't doubt that you will be victorious."

All the rebels except Jack Cade shouted, "Clifford! Clifford! We'll follow the King and Clifford."

Jack Cade thought, *Was a feather ever so lightly blown to and fro as this multitude? The name of King Henry V drags them to a hundred deeds I don't like, and it makes them leave me desolate. I see them lay their heads together as they plot to capture me. My sword must make a way for me, for there is no staying here.*

He said out loud, "In despite of the Devils and Hell, I will make my way through the middle of you! May the Heavens and honor be my witnesses that no lack of resolution in me, but only my followers' base and ignominious treasons, makes me take myself to my heels."

He dashed through the crowd of rebels and escaped.

The Duke of Buckingham said, "Has he fled? Go, some of you, and follow him. Whoever brings his head to the King shall have a thousand crowns for his reward."

Some of the rebels exited.

The Duke of Buckingham added, "Follow me, soldiers. We'll devise a way to reconcile you all to King Henry VI."

— 4.9 —

Trumpets sounded, and King Henry VI, Queen Margaret, and the Duke of Somerset, plus some attendants, appeared on the wall of Kenilworth Castle.

King Henry VI said, "Was there ever a King who enjoyed an Earthly throne and could command no more content than I? As soon as I had crept out of my cradle at nine months old, I was made a King. Never has a subject longed to be a King as I long and wish to be a subject."

The Duke of Buckingham and Lord Clifford arrived.

The Duke of Buckingham shouted to King Henry VI, "Health and glad tidings to your majesty!"

King Henry VI asked, "Buckingham, has the traitor Cade been captured? Or did he make a strategic retreat to make himself strong?"

The rebels, wearing nooses around their necks as a sign of submission, arrived.

Lord Clifford said, "Jack Cade has fled, my lord, and all his soldiers yield, and humbly so, with nooses on their necks. They await your highness' judgment of life or death."

King Henry VI said, "Then, Heaven, set open your everlasting gates to entertain my vows of thanks and praise!

"Soldiers, this day you have redeemed your lives, and showed how well you love your Prince and country. Continue always in this so good a mind, and assure yourselves that Henry, although he is unfortunate, will never be unkind. And so, with thanks and pardon to you all, I dismiss you so you can return to your different counties."

The rebels shouted, "God save the King! God save the King!"

The rebels exited.

A messenger arrived and said, "If it pleases your grace to be informed, know that the Duke of York has just come from Ireland, and with a powerful and mighty army of gallowglasses, aka heavily armed Irish soldiers, and fierce kerns, aka lightly armed Irish soldiers, he is marching here in proud array, and he continually proclaims as he comes along that his weapons are only to be used to remove from you the Duke of Somerset, whom he calls a traitor."

King Henry VI said, "Thus stands my distressed country, between Cade and York. It is like a ship that, having escaped a tempest, is immediately calmed and then boarded by a pirate.

"Just now Cade was driven back and his men dispersed, and now York has come with weapons to take Cade's place.

"I request that you, Buckingham, go and meet him, and ask him what's the reason for these weapons of his. Tell him I'll send Edmund Beaufort, the Duke of Somerset, to the Tower of London.

"Duke of Somerset, we'll commit you to the Tower until the Duke of York's army is dismissed from him."

The Duke of Somerset said, "My lord, I'll yield myself to prison willingly, or to death, to do my country good."

King Henry VI said to the Duke of Buckingham, "In any case, don't be too harsh in the discussion you have with the Duke of York, for he is fierce and cannot endure hard language."

"I will do as you say, my lord," the Duke of Buckingham replied, "and I don't doubt that I will arrange matters so that they shall turn out to be for your good."

King Henry VI said to Queen Margaret, "Come, wife, let's go in, and learn to govern better, for England may yet curse my wretched reign."

Jack Cade stood in the garden of Alexander Iden in Kent.

He said to himself, "Damn ambition! Damn myself, who has a sword, and yet is almost starved to death! These five days I have hidden in the woods outside this garden and have not dared to peep out, for all the country is looking for me, but now I am so hungry that even if I might have a lease of my life for a thousand years I still could stay no longer in the woods and starve.

"Because of my hunger, I have climbed over a brick wall into this garden to see if I can eat plants, or pick a sallet again, which is not amiss to cool a man's stomach this hot weather."

Despite his hunger, Jack Cade was able to engage in word play. The phrase "a sallet" meant both 1) a salad, and 2) a type of helmet.

He said to himself, "I think this word 'sallet' was born to do me good, for many a time, except for a sallet, my brainpan would had been cleft with a halberd, and many a time, when I have been thirsty and bravely marching, it has served me instead of a quart pot to drink in; and now the word 'sallet' must serve me to feed on."

Alexander Iden entered his garden.

Not seeing Jack Cade, he said to himself, "Lord, who would live troubled in the court, when he instead may enjoy such quiet walks as these? This small inheritance my father left me makes me content and happy, and to me it is worth a monarchy. I don't seek to grow great by other people's waning, or to gather wealth by any evil means possible. It is enough that what I have maintains my well-being and sends the poor from my gate well pleased with the alms I have given them."

Jack Cade said to himself, *Here's the lord of the soil come to seize me for a stray, for entering his fee-simple without leave.*

Alexander Iden owned the estate in fee-simple. It was his private possession in perpetuity unless he sold it. The owner of a private estate was permitted to take possession of any stray animals that wandered onto his property.

Jack Cade said to Alexander Iden, "Ah, villain, you will betray me, and get a thousand crowns from the King for carrying my head to him, but I'll make you eat iron like an ostrich, and swallow my sword like a great pin, before you and I part."

People in this culture believed that ostriches swallowed iron nails.

Alexander Iden said, "Why, rude fellow, whoever you are, I don't know you. Why, then, should I betray you? Isn't it enough to break into my garden, and, like a thief, to come to rob my grounds, climbing over my walls in spite of me the owner? Must you also defy me with these insolent words?"

Jack Cade replied, "Defy you! Yes, by the best blood — that of Christ — that ever was shed, and I will pull your beard, too. Look well at me. I have eaten no food these five days, yet if you and your five men attack me, if I do not leave you all as dead as a doornail, then I pray to God I may never eat plants anymore."

The phrase "your five men" was an insult. Jack Cade was implying that Alexander Iden had no more than five men working on his estate.

Alexander Iden said, "It shall never be said, while England stands, that Alexander Iden, an esquire of Kent, took advantage of superiority of numbers to combat a poor famished man."

An esquire held the rank of a gentleman just below that of a knight.

He continued, "Oppose your steadfast-gazing eyes to mine, and see if you can stare me down with your looks. Compare us limb to limb, and you will see that you are far the lesser. Your hand is only a finger compared to my fist. Your leg is only a stick compared with this truncheon — thick club — that is my leg. My foot shall fight with all the strength you have, and if my arm is lifted in the air, then your grave is already dug in the earth.

"As for words, whose greatness answers words, let this my sword report what speech forbears. Big words answer big words, but I will let my sword say what words cannot say."

Jack Cade replied, "By my valor, you are the most complete champion whom I ever heard!"

He then said to his sword, "Steel, if you blunt your edge, or don't cut the burly boned country boor into joints of beef before you sleep in your sheath, I will beg God on my knees that you may be melted down and turned into hobnails for shoes."

The two men fought with swords, and Alexander Iden mortally wounded Jack Cade.

Jack Cade cried, "Oh, I am slain! Famine and no one else has slain me. Let ten thousand Devils come against me, and give me just the ten meals I have not eaten the past five days, and I'll defy them all. Wither, garden, and be henceforth a cemetery to all who dwell in this house because the unconquered soul of Cade is fleeing."

Alexander Iden said, "Is it Jack Cade whom I have slain, that monstrous traitor?

"Sword, I will hallow and glorify you for this deed of yours, and I will have you hung over my tomb when I am dead. Never shall this blood be wiped from your point, but you shall wear it like a herald's red coat to emblaze and proclaim publicly like a coat of arms the honor that your master has gotten."

"Iden, farewell, and be proud of your victory," Jack Cade said. "Tell the region of Kent from me that she has lost her best man, and exhort all the people in the world to be cowards, for I, who never feared anyone, have been vanquished by famine, not by valor."

He died.

Alexander Iden said, "How much you have wronged me, let Heaven be my judge. Die, damned wretch, the curse of her who gave birth to you, and as I pierce your body with my sword" — he did just that — "so wish I that I might thrust your soul to Hell.

"I drag your corpse by the heels with your head dragging from here to a dunghill that shall be your grave, and there I will cut off your most graceless and wicked head, which I will bear in triumph to the King, leaving your trunk for crows to feed upon."

CHAPTER 5
— 5.1 —

In the fields between Dartford and Blackheath, the Duke of York and his army of Irish soldiers stood. Drummers and soldiers holding battle flags were present.

The Duke of York said to himself, "From Ireland thus come I, York, to claim my right to be King of England, and pluck the crown from feeble Henry VI's head. Ring, bells, aloud, and burn, bonfires, clear and bright, to welcome great England's lawful King.

"Ah! *Sancta majestas* — sacred majesty — who would not buy you at a high price?

"Let them obey who don't know how to rule. This hand was made to handle nothing but gold. I cannot give due action to my words, unless a sword or scepter balance my hand. My hand shall have a scepter, I swear as I have a soul, and on that scepter I'll impale the flower-de-luce — the heraldic lily — of France."

He saw the Duke of Buckingham coming toward him.

"Whom have we here?" the Duke of York asked. "Buckingham, to disturb me? The King has sent him, I am sure. I must dissemble and deceive him."

"York, if you mean well, I greet you well," the Duke of Buckingham said.

"Humphrey, Duke of Buckingham, I accept your greeting. Are you a messenger, or have you come at your own pleasure?"

"I am a messenger from King Henry VI, our dread-inspiring liege in order to learn the reason for these weapons in a time of peace, and the reason why you, being a subject as I am, against your oath and the true and loyal allegiance you have sworn, should raise so great an army without your King's leave, and the reason why you dare to bring your army so near the King's court."

The Duke of York thought, *I can scarcely speak because my anger is so great. Oh, I could hack up rocks and fight with flint because I am so angry at these abject terms he used to describe me — am I a subject! And now, like Ajax Telamonius, I could expend my fury on sheep or oxen the way he did after the armor of Achilles was awarded to Odysseus instead of to him, the rightful claimant, during the Trojan War. I am far better born than is King Henry VI. My claim to the throne is better. I am more like a King and more Kingly in my thoughts, but I must make fair weather and pretend to be friendly yet a while longer, until Henry is weaker and I am stronger.*

He said out loud, "Buckingham, I ask you to pardon me because I have given you no answer all this while. My mind was troubled with deep melancholy. The reason why I have brought this army here is to remove proud Somerset from the King. The Duke of Somerset is seditious to his grace the King and to the state."

"That is too much presumption on your part," the Duke of Buckingham said. "But if your weapons have no other purpose, know that the King has yielded to your demand: The Duke of Somerset is imprisoned in the Tower of London."

"Upon your honor, is he really a prisoner?" the Duke of York asked.

"Upon my honor, he is really a prisoner," the Duke of Buckingham replied.

The Duke of York said, "Then, Buckingham, I dismiss my army.

"Soldiers, I thank you all. Disperse yourselves. Meet me tomorrow in St. George's field. You shall have pay and everything you wish.

"And Buckingham, let my sovereign, virtuous Henry VI, be entrusted with my eldest son — no, with all my sons — as pledges of my obedience and love. I'll send them all to him as willingly as I am willing to live. Lands, goods, horses, armor, anything I have, are the King's to use, as long as the Duke of Somerset dies."

The Duke of Buckingham replied, "York, I commend and praise your kind submission. We two will go into his highness' tent."

The two men locked arms together.

King Henry VI and some attendants arrived.

The King said, "Buckingham, does York intend no harm to us? I see that he is marching with you arm in arm."

The two men unlocked arms, and the Duke of York said, "In all submission and humility, I, York, present myself to your highness."

King Henry VI said, "Then what is the purpose of these soldiers you have brought?"

The Duke of York replied, "To heave the traitor Somerset away from here, and to fight against that monstrous rebel Cade, who since I arrived I have heard to be defeated and overthrown."

Alexander Iden arrived; he was carrying Jack Cade's head.

Alexander Iden said to King Henry VI, "If one so uncultivated and of such a low condition may pass into the presence of a King, here I present to your grace a traitor's head, the head of Cade, whom I in combat slew."

"The head of Cade!" King Henry VI said. "Great God, how just You are! Oh, let me view his visage, now dead, that while living wrought me such exceeding trouble.

"Tell me, my friend, are you the man who slew him?"

"I was, if it please your majesty."

"What is your name?" King Henry VI asked. "What rank are you?"

"My name is Alexander Iden. I am a poor esquire of Kent, and I love and honor my King."

The Duke of Buckingham said, "So please it you, my lord, it is not amiss that he be created a knight as a reward for his good service."

King Henry VI said, "Iden, kneel down."

He knelt.

King Henry VI tapped Alexander Iden's shoulders with a sword and said, "Rise up a knight, Sir Alexander Iden. We give you a thousand marks as a reward, and we command that you henceforth serve us."

"May Iden live to merit such a bounty and never live otherwise than as loyal to his liege!" Sir Alexander Iden said.

Queen Margaret arrived with the Duke of Somerset, who had been imprisoned in the Tower of London.

Seeing them, King Henry VI whispered to the Duke of Buckingham, "Look, Buckingham, Somerset is coming here with the Queen. Go, tell her to hide him quickly from the Duke of York."

Queen Margaret, who had heard him, said, "He shall not hide his head on account of a thousand Yorks, but instead he will boldly stand and face him."

The Duke of York said, "What is this? Is Somerset at liberty? Then, York, unloose your long-imprisoned thoughts, and let your tongue be equal with your heart. Shall I endure the sight of Somerset?

"Lying King! Why have you broken your word to me, knowing how badly I can endure being deceived?

"Did I call you King? No, you are not a King. You are not fit to govern and rule multitudes — not you, who dare not, and cannot, rule a traitor such as the Duke of Somerset.

"That head of yours does not become a crown. Your hand was made to grasp a palmer's staff — the staff of a religious pilgrim — and not to grace an awe-inspiring Princely scepter.

"That gold crown you are wearing must round engirt these brows of mine. My smile and frown, like Achilles' spear, is able with the change to kill and cure. Achilles' spear could inflict a mortal wound and according to folklore, cure the mortal wound it inflicted. Achilles' spear wounded Telephus, and then the rust of the spear cured Telephus. My frown can kill; my smile can cure.

"Here is a hand worthy to hold a scepter up and with the same to enact controlling laws.

"Give way to me. By Heaven, you shall rule no more over me, whom Heaven created to be your ruler."

The Duke of Somerset said, "You monstrous traitor! I arrest you, York, on a charge of capital treason against the King and crown. Obey, audacious traitor; kneel for grace and mercy."

"Would you have me kneel?" the Duke of York said. "First let me ask these knees of mine if they can endure my bowing a knee to any man.

"Sirrah, call in my sons to be my bail."

One of his attendants exited.

The Duke of York continued, "I know that before they will have me go into custody, they'll pawn their swords for my freedom."

Queen Margaret ordered, "Call Clifford here! Tell him to come in all haste to say if the bastard boys of York shall be the surety for their traitor father."

The Duke of Buckingham exited.

The Duke of York said to Queen Margaret, "Oh, blood-besotted Neapolitan, outcast of Naples, England's bloody scourge!"

Queen Margaret's father was the titular King of Naples.

The Duke of York continued, "The sons of York, your betters in their birth, shall be their father's bail, and they shall be bane — ruination — to those who will refuse to allow the boys to be my surety!"

Two of his sons — Edward and Richard — entered the room. In the future, they would be King Edward IV and King Richard III.

The Duke of York said, "See where my sons are coming here. I'll warrant they'll make it good."

"Make it good" was ambiguous. It could mean 1) "be their father's bail" or 2) "be bane — ruination — to those who will refuse to allow the boys to be my surety."

Lord Clifford and his son, young Clifford, entered the room.

Queen Margaret said, "And here comes Lord Clifford to deny their bail for you."

Lord Clifford knelt before King Henry VI and said, "Health and all happiness to my lord the King!"

The Duke of York said, "I thank you, Clifford. What news do you have?"

Clifford was loyal to King Henry VI, and so he became angry when he heard the Duke of York's words.

Using the royal plural, the Duke of York said, "No, do not frighten us with an angry look. We are your sovereign, Clifford, so kneel again. We pardon you for mistakenly kneeling to Henry."

"Henry VI is my King, York," Lord Clifford angrily replied. "I have not made a mistake, but you are much mistaken if you think that I have made a mistake.

"Take this man — York — to Bedlam, the Bethlehem Hospital for the Insane in London! Has the man grown mad?"

"Yes, Clifford," King Henry VI replied. "A bedlam — insane — and ambitious disposition makes the Duke of York oppose himself against his King."

"He is a traitor," Lord Clifford said. "Let him be taken to the Tower of London, and chop away that rebellious head of his."

"He has been arrested, but he will not obey," Queen Margaret said. "His sons, he says, shall give their words and be the surety for him."

"You will, won't you, sons?" the Duke of York said to his two sons who were present.

Edward replied, "Yes, noble father, if our words will serve."

Richard added, "And if our words will not serve, then our weapons shall."

"Why, what a brood of traitors have we here!" Lord Clifford said.

"Look in a glass, and call your image a traitor," the Duke of York said. "I am your King, and you are a false-heart traitor."

He then ordered, "Call here to the stake my two brave bears, who with just the shaking of their chains may fill these dangerous-lurking curs with wonder.

"Tell Salisbury and Warwick to come to me."

The Duke of York called the Earl of Salisbury and his son, the Earl of Warwick, bears because their heraldic crest was a rampant — standing with its forefeet in the air — bear. The bear was chained to a knobby staff.

The Earl of Salisbury and the Earl of Warwick were very near and arrived immediately.

Lord Clifford said to the Duke of York, "Are these your bears? We'll bait your bears to death and manacle the bear-keeper — you — in their chains, if you dare to bring them to the baiting place."

Bear-baiting was a "sport" in which a bear was tied to a stake and then tormented by dogs.

Richard replied, "Often I have seen a hot overweening cur run back and bite its owner, because the owner was holding him back from the bear. The dog, once loose, got wounded by the bear's deadly paw and clapped its tail between its legs and yelped, and the same thing will happen to you if you oppose yourselves to and try to fight Lord Warwick."

Lord Clifford replied to Richard, "Go away, you heap of wrath, you foul improperly formed lump, you who are as crooked in your manners as in your shape!"

Richard's back was crooked as a result of scoliosis.

The Duke of York said, "We shall heat you thoroughly soon."

The heat would be the heat of battle.

"Take care, lest by your heat you burn yourselves," Lord Clifford replied.

King Henry VI said, "Why, Earl of Warwick, has your knee forgotten to bow?

"Old Earl of Salisbury, shame to your silver hair, you mad misleader of your brain-sick son! Will you on your deathbed play the ruffian, and seek for sorrow with your eyes? You are an old man and soon to die, so why seek trouble through the eyeglasses of an old man?

"Oh, where is faith? Oh, where is loyalty? If it has been banished from the frosty-haired head of an old man, where shall it find a harbor on the Earth?

"Will you go and dig a grave in seeking out war, and shame your honorable age with blood?

"Why are you old, and lack wisdom? Or why do you abuse your wisdom, if you have it?

"For shame! Out of your duty to me, bend your knee to me — your knee that is bowing to the grave with great old age."

The Earl of Salisbury said, "My lord, I have carefully considered the title and claim of this most renowned Duke of York to the throne, and in my conscience I do consider his grace to be the rightful heir to England's royal seat."

"Haven't you sworn allegiance to me?" King Henry VI asked.

"I have," the Earl of Salisbury replied.

"Can you get forgiveness from Heaven for breaking such an oath?" King Henry VI asked.

"It is a great sin to swear a sinful oath, but it is a greater sin to keep a sinful oath," the Earl of Salisbury replied. "Who can be bound by any solemn vow to do a murderous deed, to rob a man, to rape a spotless virgin and take her chastity, to bereave the orphan of his patrimony, to wring from the widow her right that is in accordance with custom to inherit part of her husband's estate, and have no other reason for this wrong except that he was bound by a solemn oath?"

Queen Margaret said, "A subtle and cunning traitor needs no sophist — no specious reasoner."

King Henry VI ordered, "Call the Duke of Buckingham, and tell him to arm himself."

The Duke of York said, "Call Buckingham and all the friends you have. I am resolved to have either death or the dignity of high office. Either I will die, or I will be King."

"The first — death — I promise you, if dreams prove to be true," Lord Clifford said.

"It is best for you to go to bed and dream again," the Earl of Warwick said. "You ought to keep yourself from the tempest of the battlefield."

Lord Clifford said, "I am resolved to bear a greater storm than any you can conjure up today, and that I'll write upon your burgonet, if I might know you by your household badge — your distinctive emblem."

A burgonet is a helmet with a visor. On top of the helmet is the family crest — the distinctive emblem of the family.

The Earl of Warwick said, "Now, by my father's badge, old Neville's crest, which is a rampant bear chained to a ragged staff, this day I'll wear it on top of my burgonet, just as on a mountain top the cedar — a symbol of royalty — stands and keeps its leaves in spite of any storm. I will do this in order to frighten you when you see my crest."

Lord Clifford replied, "And from your burgonet I'll rend your bear and tread it under foot with all contempt, despite the bear-keeper who protects the bear."

Young Clifford said, "And so let's go to arms, victorious father, to quell the rebels and their accomplices."

"Ha!" Richard said. "Show some charity! Don't be shameful! Don't speak spitefully, for you shall eat with Jesus Christ tonight."

"You foul and misshapen individual, that's more than you can know and tell," young Clifford said.

"If not in Heaven, you'll surely eat in Hell," Richard replied.

The two sides exited in different directions.

The first battle of St. Albans was taking place on 22 May 1455. At this particular location, a sign of the Castle, an inn at St. Albans, was displayed.

The Earl of Warwick said, "Lord Clifford of Cumberland, it is Warwick who is calling for you, and if you don't hide yourself from the bear, then now, as the angry trumpet sounds the battle call and dying men's cries fill the empty air, Clifford, I say, come forth and fight me.

"Proud northern lord, Clifford of Cumberland, the Earl of Warwick is hoarse with calling you to arms."

The Duke of York arrived, on foot.

Seeing him, the Earl of Warwick said, "How are you now, my noble lord? What! You are on foot!"

The Duke of York explained, "The deadly handed, death-dealing Lord Clifford slew my steed, but foe to foe I have encountered him and made a prey for carrion kites and crows out of the fine, bonny beast he loved so well."

Lord Clifford arrived.

The Earl of Warwick said to him, "For one or both of us, the time to die has come."

"Stop, Warwick," the Duke of York said, "seek out some other prey, for I myself must hunt this deer to death."

The Earl of Warwick said, "Then do so nobly, York; you are fighting for a crown.

"I intend, Lord Clifford, to thrive in battle today, and so it grieves my soul to leave you unassailed by me."

The Earl of Warwick exited.

The Duke of York looked at Lord Clifford instead of immediately fighting him.

"What is it you are seeing in me, York?" Lord Clifford asked. "Why do you pause and not begin to fight?"

"I should love your brave bearing, except that you are so firmly my enemy," the Duke of York replied.

"Your prowess ought not to lack praise and esteem," Lord Clifford said, "except it is used ignobly and treasonably."

The Duke of York said, "So let my prowess help me now against your sword as I in justice and legitimate claim to the throne express and use it."

Lord Clifford said, "I put both my soul and my body in the fight!"

"A dreadful wager! Prepare to fight immediately," the Duke of York replied.

The two fought, and the Duke of York mortally wounded Lord Clifford.

"*La fin couronne les oeuvres*," Lord Clifford said just before dying.

The French sentence meant, "The end crowns the works."

Lord Clifford meant that he had lived an honorable life and died an honorable death.

The Duke of York said, respectfully, "Thus war has given you peace, for you are still.

"May peace be with his soul, Heaven, if it be your will!"

The Duke of York exited, and young Clifford arrived.

Young Clifford said, "Shame and confusion! All the forces of King Henry VI are being routed. Fear frames disorder, and disorder wounds where it should guard — in all the confusion, we are killing our own soldiers.

"Oh, war, you son of Hell, whom the angry Heavens make their minister of vengeance, throw hot coals of vengeance in the frozen-by-fear bosoms of our army! Let no soldier flee.

"He who is truly dedicated to war has no self-love, and he who loves himself doesn't have in his own essence but only by circumstance the reputation of being a courageous person. A person who has self-love wants to stay alive."

He saw his father's corpse and said, "Oh, let the vile world end, and the preordained flames of the last day knit Earth and Heaven together! Now let the general trumpet blow its blast and proclaim that the end of the world and Doomsday — the Day of Judgment — have arrived. Let personal matters and petty sounds cease!

"Were you fated, dear father, to lose your youth in peace, and to achieve the silver livery — grey hair — of judicious, wise old age, and in your respected state and during your days in which you should be sitting in a chair, thus to die in ruffian battle?

"Now, at this sight of your corpse, my heart has turned to stone, and as long as it is mine, it shall be stony.

"The Duke of York does not spare our old men, and no more will I spare his side's babes. The tears of virgins shall be to me just like the dew is to fire."

This culture believed that drops of water made a fire hotter by turning flames into burning coals.

Young Clifford continued, "And beauty, which often subdues the tyrant, shall to my flaming wrath be oil and flax."

Oil and flax are highly flammable.

He continued, "Henceforth I will have nothing to do with pity. If I meet an infant of the House of York, I will cut it into as many pieces as wild Medea did young Absyrtus, her brother."

While fleeing in a ship with Jason, Medea murdered her young brother and cut his corpse into pieces that she dropped into the sea. Her father, who was pursuing them, stopped to collect the pieces of his son's corpse. Through this stratagem, Medea and Jason were able to escape.

Young Clifford continued, "In cruelty I will seek my fame."

He picked up the body of his father and said, "Come, you new ruin of old Clifford's house. As Aeneas bore his old father, Anchises, on his shoulders as he fled burning Troy, so I bear you upon my manly shoulders. But then Aeneas bore a living load, who was not as heavy as these woes of mine."

He exited, carrying the corpse of his father.

Richard and the Duke of Somerset arrived and began to fight.

Richard killed the Duke of Somerset and said, "So, lie there. For underneath an alehouse's paltry sign, that of the Castle in St. Albans, you, Somerset, have died and made the wizard who predicted your death famous."

Much earlier, the Duchess of Gloucester, in the presence of a witch, a conjuror (wizard), and two priests, had consulted a spirit about the Duke of Somerset. The spirit had replied, "Let him shun castles. Safer shall he be upon the sandy plains than where castles mounted stand."

Richard then said, "Sword, hold your temper. Keep your edge; stay sharp. Heart, continue to be wrathful. Priests pray for enemies, but Princes kill."

The battle continued.

King Henry VI, Queen Margaret, and their attendants knew that they had lost the battle.

Queen Margaret said to King Henry VI, "Flee, my lord! You are slow; for shame, flee away!"

"Can we outrun the Heavens and escape what God sends us?" King Henry VI asked. "Good Margaret, stay."

"What are you made of?" Queen Margaret asked, exasperated. "You'll neither fight nor flee. Manhood, wisdom, and defense all agree that the wise thing to do now is to retreat from the enemy and keep ourselves safe by whatever means we can. All we can do is flee.

"If you are captured, then we would see the lowest point of all our fortunes, but if we happen to escape, as well we may, unless your neglect and indifference to taking action keeps us from escaping, we shall go to London, where you are loved and where this breach now made in our fortunes may readily be stopped. We can recover from this defeat."

Young Clifford arrived and said, "Except that my heart is set on causing future trouble for our enemy, I would speak blasphemy before I would advise you to flee, but flee you must. Hopeless defeat reigns in the hearts of all the remaining fragments of our army.

"Flee, for your deliverance and safety! If you do so, we will live to see their day and give them our misfortune. We will live to have a day of victory like theirs and they will have a day of misfortune like ours.

"Flee, my lord, flee!"

The battle was over. Victorious, the Duke of York met with his son Richard and the Earl of Warwick. All were wearing a white rose. Soldiers, including a drummer and a soldier holding a battle flag, were present.

The Duke of York said, "Who can report what happened to the Earl of Salisbury, that lion in the winter of old age who in his rage forgets the bruises of old age and all the attacks of time, and who, like a fine fellow with the unwrinkled forehead of youth, restores himself with the opportunity to fight in a battle? This happy day is not itself — not happy — nor have we won one foot of land, if Salisbury is lost to us through death."

Richard said, "My noble father, three times today I helped him to his horse, and three times today I bestrode him to defend him. Three times today I led him away and persuaded him not to undertake any further action in the battle.

"But still, wherever danger was, there I always met him. And like rich hangings in a plain, simple, homely house, so was his will in his old feeble body.

"But, noble as he is, look at where he is coming here."

The Earl of Salisbury arrived and said to those present, "Now, by my sword, well have you fought today. By the Mass, so did we all fight well today.

"I thank you, Richard. God knows how long it is I have to live, and it has pleased Him that three times today you have defended me against imminent death.

"Well, lords, we have not got that which we have. We have won a victory, but we have not won a complete victory. It is not enough that our foes have fled this time because they are enemies who are able to regroup and to fight again."

The Duke of York said, "I know our safest course of action is to follow them, for, as I hear, the King has fled to London, to call an immediate court of Parliament. Let us pursue him before the formal orders to attend Parliament go forth.

"What does Lord Warwick advise? Shall we go after them?"

"After them?" the Earl of Warwick said. "No, before them, if we can.

"Now, by my faith, lords, it was a glorious day. St. Albans' battle won by famous York shall be famous in all ages to come.

"Let the drums and trumpets sound, and let all of us go to London, and may more such days of victory like these befall us!"

Appendix A: Brief Historical Background

KING EDWARD I: 1272-1307

Edward Longshanks fought and defeated the Welsh chieftains, and he made his eldest son the Prince of Wales. He won victories against the Scots, and he brought the coronation stone from Scone to Westminster.

KING EDWARD II: 1307-deposed 1327

At the Battle of Bannockburn in 1314, the Scots defeated his army. His wife and her lover, Mortimer, deposed him. According to legend, he was murdered in Berkeley Castle by means of a red-hot poker thrust up his anus.

KING EDWARD III: 1327-1377

Son of King Edward II, he reigned for a long time — 50 years. Because he wanted to conquer Scotland and France, he started the Hundred Years War in 1338. King Edward III and his eldest son, Edward the Black Prince, won important victories against the French in the Battle of Crécy (1346) and the Battle of Poitiers (1356).

One of King Edward III's sons was John of Gaunt, first Duke of Lancaster.

Another of King Edward III's sons was Edmund of Langley, first Duke of York.

During his reign, the Black Death — the bubonic plague — struck in 1348-1350 and killed half of England's population.

KING RICHARD II: 1377-deposed 1399

King Richard II was the son of Edward the Black Prince. In 1381, Wat Tyler led the Peasants Revolt, which was suppressed. King Richard II sent Henry, Duke of Lancaster, into exile and seized Henry's estates, but in 1399 Henry, Duke of Lancaster, returned from exile and deposed King Richard II, thereby becoming King Henry IV. In 1400, King Richard II was murdered in Pontefract Castle, which is also known as Pomfret Castle.

HOUSE OF LANCASTER

KING HENRY IV: 1399-1413

Henry, Duke of Lancaster, was the son of John of Gaunt, who was the third son of King Edward III. He was born at Bolingbroke Castle and so was also known as Henry of Bolingbroke. Returning from exile in France to reclaim his estates, he deposed King Richard II. He spent the 13 years of his reign putting down rebellions and defending himself against those who would assassinate or depose him. The Welshman Owen Glendower and the English Percy family were among those who fought against him. King Henry IV died at the age of 45.

KING HENRY V: 1413-1422

The son of King Henry IV, King Henry V renewed the war with France. He and his army defeated the French at the Battle of Agincourt (1415) despite being heavily outnumbered. He married Catherine of Valoise, the daughter of the French King, but he died before becoming King of France. He left behind a 10-month-old son, who became King Henry VI.

KING HENRY VI: 1422-deposed 1461; briefly returned to the throne in 1470-1471

The Hundred Years War ended in 1453; the English lost all land in France except for Calais, a port city. After King Henry VI suffered an attack of mental illness in 1454, Richard, third Duke of York and the father of King Henry IV and King Richard III, was made Protector of the Realm. England suffered civil war after the House of York challenged King Henry VI's right to be King of England. In 1470, King Henry VI was briefly restored to the English throne. In 1471, he was murdered in the Tower of London. A short time previously, his son, Edward, Prince of Wales, had been killed at the Battle of Tewkesbury in 1471; this was the final battle in the Wars of the Roses. The Yorkists decisively defeated the Lancastrians.

King Henry VI founded both Eton College and King's College, Cambridge.

WARS OF THE ROSES

From 1455-1487, the Yorkists and the Lancastrians fought for power in England in the famous Wars of the Roses. The emblem of the York family was a white rose, and the emblem of the Lancaster family was a red rose. The Yorkists and the Lancastrians were descended from King Edward III.

HOUSE OF YORK

KING EDWARD IV: 1461-1483 (King Henry VI briefly returned to the throne in 1470-1471)

Son of Richard, third Duke of York, he charged his brother George, Duke of Clarence, with treason and had him murdered in 1478. After dying suddenly, he left behind two sons aged 12 and 9, and five daughters.

His surviving two brothers in Shakespeare's play *Richard III* are these: 1) George, Duke of Clarence. Clarence is the second-oldest brother; and 2) Richard, Duke of Gloucester, and afterwards King Richard III. Gloucester is the youngest surviving brother.

William Caxton established the first printing press in Westminster during King Edward IV's reign.

KING EDWARD V: 1483-1483

The eldest son of King Edward IV, he reigned for only two months, the shortest-lived monarch in English history. He was 13 years old. He and his younger brother, Richard, were murdered in the Tower of London. According to Shakespeare's play, their uncle, Richard, Duke of Gloucester, who became King Richard III, was responsible for their murders.

KING RICHARD III: 1483-1485

Brother of King Edward IV, Richard, the Duke of Gloucester, declared the two Princes in the Tower of London — King Edward V and Richard, Duke of York — illegitimate and made himself King Richard III. In 1485, Henry Tudor, Earl of Richmond, a descendant of John of Gaunt, who was the father of King Henry IV, defeated King Richard III at the Battle of Bosworth Field in Leicestershire. King Richard III died in that battle.

King Richard III's father was Richard Plantagenet, Duke of York. His mother was Cecily Neville, Duchess of York.

King Richard III's death in the Battle of Bosworth Field is regarded as marking the end of the Middle Ages in England.

A NOTE ON THE PLANTAGENETS

The first Plantagenet King was King Henry II (1154-1189). From 1154 until 1485, when King Richard III died, all English Kings were Plantagenets. Both the Lancaster family and the York family were Plantagenets.

Geoffrey Plantagenet, Count of Anjou, was the founder of the House of Plantagenet. Geoffrey's son, Henry Curtmantle, became King Henry II of England, thereby founding the Plantagenet dynasty. Geoffrey wore a sprig of broom, a flowering shrub, as a badge; the Latin name for broom is *planta genista*, and from it the name "Plantagenet" arose.

The Plantagenet dynasty can be divided into three parts:

1154-1216: The Angevins. The Angevin Kings were Henry II, Richard I (Richard the Lionheart), and John 1.

1216-1399: The Plantagenets. These Kings ranged from King Henry III to King Richard II.

1399-1485: The Houses of Lancaster and of York. These Kings ranged from King Henry IV to King Richard III.

BEGINNING OF THE TUDOR DYNASTY

KING HENRY VII: 1485-1509

When King Richard III fell at the Battle of Bosworth, Henry Tudor, Earl of Richmond, became King Henry VII. A Lancastrian, he married Elizabeth of York — young Elizabeth of York in *Richard III* — and united the two warring houses, York and Lancaster, thus ending the Wars of the Roses. One of his grandfathers was Sir Owen Tudor, who married Catherine of Valoise, widow of King Henry V.

KING HENRY VIII: 1509-1547

King Henry VIII had six wives. These are their fates: "Divorced, Beheaded, Died, Divorced, Beheaded, Survived." He divorced his first wife, Catherine of Aragon, so that he could marry Anne Boleyn. Because of this, England divorced itself from the Catholic Church, and King Henry VIII became the head of the Church of England. King Henry VIII had one son and two daughters, all of whom became rulers of England: Edward, daughter of Jane Seymour; Mary, daughter of Catherine of Aragon; and Elizabeth, daughter of Anne Boleyn.

KING EDWARD VI: 1547-1553

The son of Henry VIII and Jane Seymour, King Edward VI succeeded his father at the age of nine; a Council of Regency with his uncle, Duke of Somerset, styled Protector, ruled the government.

During King Edward VI's reign, Archbishop Thomas Cranmer wrote the 1549 Book of Common Prayer.

When King Edward VI died, Lady Jane Grey was proclaimed Queen, but she ruled for only nine days before being executed in 1554, aged 17. Mary, daughter of Catherine of Aragon, became Queen. She was Catholic, thus the attempt to make Lady Jane Grey, a Protestant, Queen.

QUEEN MARY I (BLOODY MARY) 1553-1558

Queen Mary I attempted to make England a Catholic nation again. Some Protestant bishops, including Archbishop Thomas Cranmer, were burnt at the stake, and other violence broke out, resulting in her being known as Bloody Mary.

QUEEN ELIZABETH I: 1558-1603

The daughter of King Henry VIII and Anne Boleyn, Queen Elizabeth I was a popular Queen. In 1588, the English navy decisively defeated the Spanish Armada. England had many notable playwrights and poets, including William Shakespeare and Ben Jonson, during her reign. She never married and had no children.

KING JAMES I OF ENGLAND: A MEMBER OF THE HOUSE OF STUART

KING JAMES I OF ENGLAND AND VI OF SCOTLAND: 1603-1625

King James I of England was the son of Mary, Queen of Scots, and Lord Darnley. In 1605 Guy Fawkes and his Catholic co-conspirators were captured before they could blow up the Houses of Parliament; this was known as the Gunpowder Plot.

In 1611, during King James I's reign, the Authorized Version of the Bible (the King James Version) was completed.

Also during King James I's reign, in 1620 the Pilgrims sailed for America in their ship *The Mayflower*.

A NOTE ON SHAKESPEARE

William Shakespeare lived under two monarchs: Queen Elizabeth I and King James I.

Appendix B: About the Author

It was a dark and stormy night. Suddenly a cry rang out, and on a hot summer night in 1954, Josephine, wife of Carl Bruce, gave birth to a boy — me. Unfortunately, this young married couple allowed Reuben Saturday, Josephine's brother, to name their first-born. Reuben, aka "The Joker," decided that Bruce was a nice name, so he decided to name me Bruce Bruce. I have gone by my middle name — David — ever since.

Being named Bruce David Bruce hasn't been all bad. Bank tellers remember me very quickly, so I don't often have to show an ID. It can be fun in charades, also. When I was a counselor as a teenager at Camp Echoing Hills in Warsaw, Ohio, a fellow counselor gave the signs for "sounds like" and "two words," then she pointed to a bruise on her leg twice. Bruise Bruise? Oh yeah, Bruce Bruce is the answer!

Uncle Reuben, by the way, gave me a haircut when I was in kindergarten. He cut my hair short and shaved a small bald spot on the back of my head. My mother wouldn't let me go to school until the bald spot grew out again.

Of all my brothers and sisters (six in all), I am the only transplant to Athens, Ohio. I was born in Newark, Ohio, and have lived all around Southeastern Ohio. However, I moved to Athens to go to Ohio University and have never left.

At Ohio U, I never could make up my mind whether to major in English or Philosophy, so I got a bachelor's degree with a double major in both areas, then I added a master's degree in English and a master's degree in Philosophy.

Currently, and for a long time to come (I eat fruits and veggies), I am spending my retirement writing books such as *Nadia Comaneci: Perfect 10*, *The Funniest People in Dance*, Homer's *Iliad: A Retelling in Prose*, and William Shakespeare's *Othello: A Retelling in Prose*.

By the way, my sister Brenda Kennedy writes romances such as *A New Beginning* and *Shattered Dreams*.

Appendix C: Some Books by David Bruce

Retellings of a Classic Work of Literature

Arden of Faversham: *A Retelling*

Ben Jonson's The Alchemist: *A Retelling*

Ben Jonson's The Arraignment, or Poetaster: *A Retelling*

Ben Jonson's Bartholomew Fair: *A Retelling*

Ben Jonson's The Case is Altered: *A Retelling*

Ben Jonson's Catiline's Conspiracy: *A Retelling*

Ben Jonson's The Devil is an Ass: *A Retelling*

Ben Jonson's Epicene: *A Retelling*

Ben Jonson's Every Man in His Humor: *A Retelling*

Ben Jonson's Every Man Out of His Humor: *A Retelling*

Ben Jonson's The Fountain of Self-Love, or Cynthia's Revels: *A Retelling*

Ben Jonson's The Magnetic Lady, or Humors Reconciled: *A Retelling*

Ben Jonson's The New Inn, or The Light Heart: *A Retelling*

Ben Jonson's Sejanus' Fall: *A Retelling*

Ben Jonson's The Staple of News: *A Retelling*

Ben Jonson's A Tale of a Tub: *A Retelling*

Ben Jonson's Volpone, or the Fox: *A Retelling*

Christopher Marlowe's Complete Plays: Retellings

Christopher Marlowe's Dido, Queen of Carthage: *A Retelling*

Christopher Marlowe's Doctor Faustus: *Retellings of the 1604 A-Text and of the 1616 B-Text*

Christopher Marlowe's Edward II: *A Retelling*

Christopher Marlowe's The Massacre at Paris: *A Retelling*

Christopher Marlowe's The Rich Jew of Malta: *A Retelling*

Christopher Marlowe's Tamburlaine, Parts 1 and 2: *Retellings*

Dante's Divine Comedy: *A Retelling in Prose*

Dante's Inferno: *A Retelling in Prose*

Dante's Purgatory: *A Retelling in Prose*

Dante's Paradise: *A Retelling in Prose*

The Famous Victories of Henry V: *A Retelling*

From the Iliad *to the* Odyssey: *A Retelling in Prose of Quintus of Smyrna's* Posthomerica

George Chapman, Ben Jonson, and John Marston's Eastward Ho! *A Retelling*

George Peele's The Arraignment of Paris: *A Retelling*

George Peele's The Battle of Alcazar: *A Retelling*

George Peele's David and Bathsheba, and the Tragedy of Absalom: *A Retelling*

George Peele's Edward I: *A Retelling*

George Peele's The Old Wives' Tale: *A Retelling*

George-a-Greene: *A Retelling*

"

William Shakespeare's 1 Henry IV, aka Henry IV, Part 1: *A Retelling in Prose*

William Shakespeare's 2 Henry IV, aka Henry IV, Part 2: *A Retelling in Prose*

William Shakespeare's 1 Henry VI, aka Henry VI, Part 1: *A Retelling in Prose*

William Shakespeare's 2 Henry VI, aka Henry VI, Part 2: *A Retelling in Prose*

William Shakespeare's 3 Henry VI, aka Henry VI, Part 3: *A Retelling in Prose*

William Shakespeare's All's Well that Ends Well: *A Retelling in Prose*

William Shakespeare's Antony and Cleopatra: *A Retelling in Prose*

William Shakespeare's As You Like It: *A Retelling in Prose*

William Shakespeare's The Comedy of Errors: *A Retelling in Prose*

William Shakespeare's Coriolanus: *A Retelling in Prose*

William Shakespeare's Cymbeline: *A Retelling in Prose*

William Shakespeare's Hamlet: *A Retelling in Prose*

William Shakespeare's Henry V: *A Retelling in Prose*

William Shakespeare's Henry VIII: *A Retelling in Prose*

William Shakespeare's Julius Caesar: *A Retelling in Prose*

William Shakespeare's King John: *A Retelling in Prose*

William Shakespeare's King Lear: *A Retelling in Prose*

William Shakespeare's Love's Labor's Lost: *A Retelling in Prose*

William Shakespeare's Macbeth: *A Retelling in Prose*

William Shakespeare's Measure for Measure: *A Retelling in Prose*

William Shakespeare's The Merchant of Venice: *A Retelling in Prose*

William Shakespeare's The Merry Wives of Windsor: *A Retelling in Prose*

William Shakespeare's A Midsummer Night's Dream: *A Retelling in Prose*

William Shakespeare's Much Ado About Nothing: *A Retelling in Prose*

William Shakespeare's Othello: *A Retelling in Prose*

William Shakespeare's Pericles, Prince of Tyre: *A Retelling in Prose*

William Shakespeare's Richard II: *A Retelling in Prose*

William Shakespeare's Richard III: *A Retelling in Prose*

William Shakespeare's Romeo and Juliet: *A Retelling in Prose*

William Shakespeare's The Taming of the Shrew: *A Retelling in Prose*

William Shakespeare's The Tempest: *A Retelling in Prose*

William Shakespeare's Timon of Athens: *A Retelling in Prose*

William Shakespeare's Titus Andronicus: *A Retelling in Prose*

William Shakespeare's Troilus and Cressida: *A Retelling in Prose*

William Shakespeare's Twelfth Night: *A Retelling in Prose*

William Shakespeare's The Two Gentlemen of Verona: *A Retelling in Prose*

William Shakespeare's The Two Noble Kinsmen: *A Retelling in Prose*

William Shakespeare's The Winter's Tale: *A Retelling in Prose*